Do you have a Matchmaking Mother from Hell? Take our test and find out... if you dare.

1) Your mother always wanted you to grow up to be:
a) A model, or in any other profession where you would make a decent salary.
b) A nun.
c) A wife—anybody's wife!

2) Your mom's perfect son-in-law would be:
a) A lawyer, or in any other profession where he would make a decent salary.
b) A foreign delegate who would make it home once every five years.
c) Anybody *except* the drop-dead-gorgeous guy who just happens to be the son of her worst enemy.

3) You would spend your honeymoon:
a) On a tropical island in the Pacific.
b) In a run-down shack in the Ozarks.
c) Trying to keep your mother from killing your mother-in-law!

If you chose A most often: You have it made. Your mother seems to *actually* want what's best for you. But then again, maybe she's just planning for her retirement.

If you chose B most often: Look at the bright side—at least your mom isn't a matchmaker.

If you chose C most often: Run for the hills. But don't be surprised to find your mother hot on your trail, with a stream of eligible (but undesirable) bachelors behind her.

Dear Reader,

Spring is the season for love! LOVE & LAUGHTER celebrates with another month of romantic comedies that tickle the funny bone and reveal more than a few truths about falling in love!

Our Matchmaking Moms (from Hell) miniseries continues with *One Mom Too Many* by always popular and talented Vicki Lewis Thompson. This delightful tale has two moms with marriage on their minds—for their kids. Little do they suspect they have done their work too well....

We also welcome another new author, Bonnie Tucker, to LOVE & LAUGHTER. In *Hannah's Hunks* the heroine, Hannah, is a caterer who can't find her way around a kitchen, but cooks up a mess of trouble when she runs into undercover agent Chance McCoy. He's investigating everyone in the small, serene town of Sugar Land, most especially the beautiful caterer who can't cook and seems to be running an undercover operation of her own.

Have a few laughs on us!

Malle Vallik

Malle Vallik
Associate Senior Editor

ONE MOM TOO MANY
Vicki Lewis Thompson

Harlequin Books

TORONTO • NEW YORK • LONDON
AMSTERDAM • PARIS • SYDNEY • HAMBURG
STOCKHOLM • ATHENS • TOKYO • MILAN
MADRID • WARSAW • BUDAPEST • AUCKLAND

ISBN 0-373-44017-0

ONE MOM TOO MANY

"My recent trip to Ireland inspired me to write the story of Maureen and Bridget, the battling Irish moms," says **Vicki Lewis Thompson**. "I also got to experience Driving on the Wrong Side of the Road. Ten minutes away from the rental car office, I shredded a tire (tyre) on the left-hand curb. A soft-spoken man cheerfully fixed it and I continued on my white-knuckled way. But the curbs weren't always available for gauging my position, and I'm a teensy bit afraid that while driving through the narrow streets of Tralee, I might have nudged an Irishman's foot. His backward leap was a subtle indication that I had. I would have gone back to check on him, but I was quickly caught up in a roundabout, and shot off in a new direction. However, it is with great pride that I tell you that when I returned the car, the left-hand mirror was still attached!"

Books by Vicki Lewis Thompson

HARLEQUIN LOVE & LAUGHTER
5—STUCK WITH YOU

HARLEQUIN TEMPTATION
555—THE TRAILBLAZER
559—THE DRIFTER
563—THE LAWMAN
600—HOLDING OUT FOR A HERO
624—MR. VALENTINE

A toast to the lads of Dan Foley's Bar.

And many thanks to Ann Farwell Taylor, my stalwart companion during our Excellent Irish Adventure, and to Sue Engel, owner of Singing Swords Irish Wolfhound Kennels, for her invaluable information about this amazing breed. Any mistakes regarding Irish wolfhounds are mine and not Sue's.

1

"JUST SUPPOSE YOUR sperm loses motility," Maureen O'Malley called to her son from the kitchen where she was tending a pot of Irish stew.

"What?" Daniel almost dropped the picture frame in his hand as he whirled from his examination of the family photos on the mantel. Surely the noise of Brooklyn traffic outside the apartment window had made him misunderstand his mother. She couldn't have been talking about his sperm.

"Motility. How fast the little buggers can swim." His mother came to the kitchen doorway, a flowered apron over her expansive middle and a ladle in one hand. Other than the shocking shade of red she dyed her hair, she looked like a middle-aged matron out of a Hallmark commercial, but she sure as hell wasn't talking like one. "Did you know you could lose that, Daniel?"

He eased a finger around the back of his collar. The room was way too warm all of a sudden. "Look, Mom, I don't think—"

"Happens with age, it does." She pointed the ladle at him. "I read it in *Prevention* magazine. If you don't watch out, it could happen to you, Mr. I-don't-want-to-get-married-yet."

Daniel clenched his jaw. Ever since his father died his mother had been on this kick, and he'd about had it. In his more sympathetic moments, he understood her need to enlarge the family that suddenly seemed too small, and he'd vowed months ago to remain patient even as he refused to fall in with her timetable. Patience was getting harder to come by.

Discussing his sperm count was a new tactic, and he definitely didn't want her going any farther down that road. He took refuge in the first thing at hand. He held up the picture frame. "What's up with this, Mom?"

"You're changing the subject."

"It needed changing. How come you have this on the mantel when nothing's in it but the picture stuck in there by the frame company?"

His mother looked uncomfortable and her Irish brogue grew more prominent. "Reminded me of Bridget Hogan, is all. So I bought it."

"Bridget? Wasn't she your bitter enemy?"

"Well, she was, indeed. But before that, she was my best friend. Never had another. That woman in the frame is the spitting image of her."

"Is she, now?" Daniel held the picture up and looked more closely at the model in the photograph. Ringlets of soft auburn hair fell gracefully around delicate shoulders. Kissable red lips framed even white teeth, and the sparkle in the woman's green gaze gave new meaning to the clichéd words of the old song "When Irish Eyes are Smiling." For if she wasn't Irish, she could certainly pass.

Daniel was touched by his mother's impulse to buy the frame just because of the picture in it. Probably just another example of how lonely she'd become in her widowhood. He walked over and positioned the photograph exactly as she'd had it before, right next to the one of him after he'd graduated from the New York City Police Academy.

His mother came over to study the two adjacent pictures. "You look good with that model."

"Of course I do. She's a professional beauty. She'd make any guy look good."

His mother swatted his arm. "'Twas not what I meant. I meant you two would make a nice couple."

Daniel blew out his breath in exasperation. "Could we agree not to talk about that anymore tonight? I just turned thirty-three, for God's sake. Dad didn't marry you until he was thirty-five."

"And you see what happened. We were only blessed once."

Daniel put an arm around her shoulders, hoping to kid her out of her preoccupation. "What's the matter, aren't you happy with the one you've got?"

"I think you're lovely, and well you know it. But I'd thought to have a nursery full of babes." She sighed. "I realize now your dear, departed father probably had slow sperm."

Daniel snorted. Slow sperm was obviously Maureen O'Malley's current health-news preoccupation. Last week it had been the carcinogens from aluminum cooking pots.

"Laugh all you like. 'Tis a fact of life, and time is running out for you. Just remember that a man with no wife and children is like a boot with no laces."

He gave her a quick hug. "Exactly. Free to be loose and comfortable."

She pulled away and glared at him. "Daniel Patrick O'Malley, I did not raise you to toy with the hearts of young girls. 'Tis past time for you to pick out some lucky lass and ask her to be your wife. Surely there's someone you fancy."

This was one stubborn woman, Daniel thought wearily. He'd gained new respect for his father's patience in dealing with her all those years. "Well, come to think of it, there is someone," he said, guiding her back toward the kitchen.

"I knew you'd been holding out on me! Who is she? The one you took to the Policemen's Ball? No, wait. I'll wager 'tis the one you met at that New Year's Eve party."

"Nope." He grinned at her, quite sure his answer was a safe one. "That girl in the picture frame. She's exactly what I'm looking for."

"WHAT DO YOU THINK, St. Paddy? Shall I call Maureen O'Malley or not?" Rose Kingsford lifted the cloth muzzle of her Irish wolfhound, a stuffed animal version of the dog she hoped someday to own. St. Paddy, created slightly smaller than a live wolfhound, stared back at her with soulful brown eyes. "Can't resist a mystery, can you, pup? Okay, I'll call her. It's safe enough to do that, I think."

The stuffed animal draped over her shoulder, Rose went in search of her portable phone. She longed for a real dog, but as long as she lived in a New York City high-rise, keeping an animal the size of a wolfhound seemed criminally selfish.

But Rose didn't intend to spend the rest of her life in an apartment. An apartment was no place for a big dog or a growing child, and she intended to have both. At one point she'd thought a husband would be part of the mix, but she'd finally abandoned that dream. Most men focused so exclusively on her looks that she'd never trust them to stick around when gray hair and wrinkles showed up.

Aside from that, she'd dated fun-loving men with no maturity, and serious types with no gift for play. A combination of mature self-confidence and playfulness seemed nonexistent, and after the way her parents' marriage had turned out, she'd decided to settle for just having a child.

She'd always longed for the creative role of parenting a son or daughter, and she was afraid of becoming too set in her solitary ways if she didn't act soon.

If necessary she'd go to a sperm bank, but she'd rather ask a willing donor she'd met and screened herself—someone with no interest in a commitment, someone with intelligence and reasonably good looks, someone with no life-threatening genetic flaws. So far, no good candidate had presented himself, but Rose had trusted in her instincts for most of her thirty years. When the right man came along, she'd know.

She located the phone on her drafting table under a stack of Sunday comic pages from all over the country. "Guard my stuff, Paddy," she instructed, plopping the dog on her stool as she picked up the phone and returned to the living room.

After switching on a lamp against the twilight, Rose pulled up the antenna on the phone and dialed the number. Then she stretched out on her chintz sofa and propped her long legs over the back cushions. Probably some creative sales scheme, she thought as the phone rang. Balancing the phone between her cheek and her shoulder, she pulled her long red hair into a ponytail and wound it with a scrunchy.

"Hello?" said a musical, feminine voice.

Rose sat up straighter. No answering machine at the O'Malley residence, which was unusual in today's world. And Maureen O'Malley's voice, if that was the woman who'd answered, contained the same lilt as Rose's mother's. Perhaps Maureen had been born in Ireland. Rose was always on the lookout for material for her fledgling comic strip, her ticket out of the modeling business. "May I speak to Maureen O'Malley, please?" she asked.

"'Tis her you have."

Rose warmed to the soft brogue. Maureen sounded even more Irish than Rose's mother, who had been coached by her English husband to give up some of her native inflections.

She adjusted the phone against her ear. "This is Rose Kingsford. You contacted the modeling agency about me, I believe."

"Oh! I did indeed! So 'tis Rose, then? What a lovely name. An Irish name, for sure. Do you have Irish in your background, then?"

"On my mother's side." Upon hearing the familiar cadence of an Irish-born woman's speech, Rose instinctively let down her guard. "My father's English." And her mother now referred to him as "that Brit bastard I married."

"I knew you must be Irish! I saw that face and said to myself, 'That's an Irish lass for sure.' And I was right."

Rose reached for a pen and pad of paper she kept handy on the coffee table. This conversation could yield some homespun expressions she might be able to use in the comic strip. "Is there something I can do for you, Mrs. O'Malley?" She took a guess at the woman's marital status because she didn't feel comfortable calling someone from her mother's generation by her first name.

"Oh, Rose, there is. There most certainly is. 'Twould do me so much good to lay eyes on you. Some tea, perhaps. I know you're very busy, but it would mean so much."

Rose stopped doodling on the pad as warnings sounded in her head. This was why she guarded her privacy so carefully. Her face and figure might be out there for public consumption, but she remained personally elusive, unreachable. Crazies were everywhere, and more than one of her modeling friends had attracted a stalker. Rose cleared her throat. "I am very busy, Mrs. O'Malley, and I'm afraid that I can't—"

"But you see, you're the exact likeness of my dear friend Bridget, who threw herself off the Cliffs of Moher and drowned herself. I've been missing her for thirty-seven years, come this summer."

Rose's mouth dropped open. Her mother's name was Bridget. And her mother had once told Rose a story about a long-lost friend who had thrown herself in front of a train some thirty-seven years ago. A friend by the name of…Maureen. This had to be more than coincidence. Feeling as if she'd entered some twilight zone, Rose chose her words carefully. "I'll have to, uh, check my schedule, Mrs. O'Malley. Could I get back to you on this in, say, twenty-four hours?"

"Oh, 'twould be grand, Rose. I'll be waiting for your call, I will."

"Right. Goodbye, now." Rose pushed the disconnect button on her phone, got the dial tone back and punched in her mother's number. Her mother's machine came on, and Bridget Kingsford's intonations were very similar to Maureen O'Malley's. Rose knew her mother was probably home and screening her calls. "Put the kettle on, Mom," she instructed. "I'm on my way."

BRIDGET HOGAN KINGSFORD'S third-floor apartment looked out on Central Park. The apartment and a generous monthly allowance had been part of the settlement from Cecil Kingsford when he'd dumped his wife of twenty-five years for a younger, better-educated, smoother-skinned trophy wife. The divorce had presented Rose with a harsh example of what could happen when a man married a woman primarily for her beauty.

Rose used her key and called out a greeting as she

opened the door to the apartment. The muffled, muted re-sponse told her to look for her mother in the bedroom. She walked into the Victorian room of lace and flowers and found her mother, dressed in a pale blue jogging suit, lying on the floor with her feet propped vertically against the pink-striped wall. Her face was covered with a hardening lime-green mask.

"Well, if it isn't Freddy Krueger," Rose said, plopping to the floor next to her.

"Don't make me laugh," her mother said, barely moving her lips.

"I have some news that just might crack that thing right off your face. How much longer before you can wash it off?"

Bridget picked up the egg timer from the floor beside her and looked at it. "Eight minutes."

"Have you eaten?"

"Nope."

"Me neither." Rose pushed herself to her feet. "I'll go nuke a couple of Lean Cuisines and put on some tea."

Ten minutes later when Bridget appeared in the kitchen with her face scrubbed clean and her short auburn hair brushed softly around her face, Rose thought she looked at least twenty years younger than her actual age of fifty-six. Cecil Kingsford was a fool for sure.

"So what's this news?" her mother said as she got out Wedgwood cups and saucers for the tea.

Rose scraped the second Lean Cuisine onto a plate and carried both servings to the linen-covered table in the small dining area just beyond the kitchen. "You might want to come and sit down first."

The cups rattled in their saucers as her mother set them quickly on the counter. "My God, you've gotten yourself pregnant!"

"No, no. That's not it. Nothing to do with that."

Abandoning the serving of tea, Bridget stomped into the dining area, her hands on her hips. A frown creased the forehead she'd been working so hard to smooth with the clay mask. "Then I suppose you've found a 'candidate' for this unholy plan of yours. Rose Erin Kingsford, I don't know how I failed, that you would even consider having a babe out of wedlock. Your grandmother Hogan would turn over in her grave."

"Mom, this has nothing to do with me getting pregnant. I'm not sure I'm going to do that, anyway," she hedged, regretting once again that she'd ever confided her plan to her mother. "Please, bring the tea and I'll tell you all about my news."

Bridget brought the tea on a little tray along with the Wedgwood teapot, creamer and sugar bowl. Had her mother not always served tea with such ceremony, Rose might have thought the formality was designed to remind her daughter of the proprieties. Deep down, Bridget Kingsford, despite her apparently modern attitudes, was an Irish country girl who believed in chastity before marriage, not to mention legitimate offspring.

Bridget settled herself in her chair, placed her napkin in her lap and poured the tea. Then she carefully doctored hers with cream and sugar before glancing up. "Well? Am I sufficiently calm now, do you suppose? Or would you prefer me lying down?"

Rose laughed. Thank goodness her mother was so feisty. Otherwise, the divorce would have broken her. Rose picked up her tea and took a sip, which was wonderful, as always. Nobody could make a pot of tea like Bridget Kingsford. "I returned a call today from a woman named Maureen O'Malley. She contacted the agency because she was attracted by my picture, the one the frame company's using."

"I'm not surprised. That's a lovely shot of you."

"So she said. Reminded her of a girlhood friend who'd thrown herself off the Cliffs of Moher." Rose took a bite of her dinner, watching her mother's face.

"Good heavens!"

Rose chewed and swallowed. "She said her friend's name was Bridget." Her mother's green eyes widened and two spots of color appeared on her cheeks. "Tell me again what the woman's name was who called the agency."

"Maureen."

Her mother threw her napkin to the table and leaped up. "It's her! She should have the Blarney Stone welded to her lips!" Bridget paced the dining area and waved both arms. "How dare she go around saying I leaped off the Cliffs of Moher! But what else could I expect from the likes of her?"

Rose refrained from mentioning that the woman whom her mother had claimed had thrown herself in front of a speeding train was alive and living in Brooklyn.

Bridget spun to face her daughter. "Does she know who you are?"

"I'm not sure. She didn't sound as if she had the slightest clue. She wants to meet me, though."

Bridget clutched her head with both hands. "Let me think, let me think. Mark my words, she has something up her sleeve. You can't trust that one farther than you can toss a haywagon. Why would she want to meet you if she doesn't know you're my daughter?"

"I really don't know. Just exactly what happened between you two, Mom?"

"What happened? She ruined the biggest chance of my

life. Kept me from winning the Rose of Tralee crown. May her children have warts on their hindmost parts.''

Rose smothered a grin. When her mother became agitated she slipped into the most wonderfully colorful language. ''You never told me exactly how she kept you from winning the crown.''

Her mother threw up an arm in a dramatic gesture. ''*She* had the brilliant idea that we were too white-skinned, that we needed a kiss of sun on our cheeks before the judging. She rented a tanning lamp and I bought the suntan oil. But at the last minute my saintèd mother, may she rest in peace, talked me out of it. I took the tanning oil over to Maureen, because she insisted on doing it, anyway. And she burned her face something terrible. Had to drop out of the contest altogether.''

''So how did that stop you from winning?''

''I will tell you.'' Bridget lifted her chin, a picture of wronged innocence. ''Personality counts as much as beauty in that contest, and Maureen spread the word that I'd deliberately sabotaged her because I was afraid of the competition! As if that sheep-faced woman ever had a chance. But those fools of judges must have believed her, because I didn't win.''

Rose shook her head. It seemed that thirty-seven years hadn't dimmed her mother's memory, or her fury. She couldn't help but ask now, ''How come each of you claimed the other committed suicide?''

Her mother had the good grace to look uncomfortable at being caught in an outright lie. ''The last time we saw each other, she shouted at me 'You might as well be dead, Bridget Mary Hogan!' So I shouted back 'Same to you, Maureen Fiona Keegan!' She took a position as a nanny here in New York, and about a year later I came over to work as a model. I didn't like thinking of her in the same city as me, so I made up a story about her throwing herself in front of a train."

"And she had you taking a swan dive off the Cliffs of Moher."

"Which is ridiculous! She knows I'm terribly afraid of high places." Bridget continued to pace. "She *must* suspect who you are."

"I don't think so, Mom. But it doesn't matter. I have no intention of meeting her."

Bridget faced her. "Oh, but you must! I want to know how she turned out!"

"You *want* me to meet this woman you hate?"

"I do, indeed." Bridget gazed out the window and tapped her finger against her lips. "That little tearoom on Forty-sixth is perfect. You can sit on one side of that planter <u>and</u> I'll sit on the other. She'll never see me through the dieffenbachia."

Rose nearly lost it. "You're going to hide in the greenery and spy on her? Tell me you're not."

Her mother crossed her arms and gave Rose a look that might have come from a nineteen-year-old. "If I know Maureen Keegan, and I certainly do know that bag of wind, she's up to something. I intend to find out exactly what it is."

SOMEWHERE ALONG the line, Rose thought as she headed for the tearoom two days later, she'd switched roles with her mother. Rose was now expected to be the responsible one while her mother cavorted around like some giddy teenager concocting elaborate schemes to thwart her girlhood rival. An episode of "Mission: Impossible" hadn't been given this much thought or preparation. Everything had been planned down to the last detail, including a hat and sunglasses for her mother, in case somehow Maureen might recognize her.

According to the timetable Bridget was already in the tearoom, and whichever side of the planter she'd managed to secure for herself, Rose was supposed to get a table on the other side. Maureen wasn't scheduled to arrive for another fifteen minutes, so Rose and Bridget would have time to jockey for position in case other patrons had seated themselves in ways that would louse up the Plan.

Rose stepped into the warmth of the tearoom and unbuttoned her trench coat as she approached the hostess. "I have a reservation for two. The name is Kingsford."

"Right this way." Carrying menus, the hostess led her into the delicately appointed room featuring antiques from the turn of the century.

Rose spotted her mother with her back to the door, looking like Mata Hari in her broad-brimmed hat of navy wool pulled low over her dark glasses. The hostess was heading for the table right behind her, on the same side of the planter. On the other side, the tables were filled. Rose sighed. Then she touched the hostess on the shoulder. "I'm afraid this will be a terrible bother, but I have a strange request regarding my table."

Rose's mother stiffened at the sound of her daughter's voice.

The hostess turned with a smile that looked totally insincere. "What can I do for you?"

"The person I'm meeting is very sentimental, and she has fond memories of that table over there." Rose pointed to a table on the opposite side of the planter and directly across from where her mother was sipping a cup of tea.

"Customers are occupying that table."

"I can see that, but if they could possibly be persuaded to move..." Rose gave the hostess her most soulful look, something approximating the expression of her stuffed dog St. Paddy. Then she slipped a folded twenty into the hostess's hand.

The hostess glanced at the denomination of the bill. "Perhaps that can be arranged," she murmured. "Just give me a moment."

Rose glanced at her watch and hoped a moment wasn't very long with this chick. The hostess had less than ten moments to get Rose seated or the whole program would collapse. Rose hoped Maureen wasn't the sort of woman who arrived early.

The two women who'd been asked to relocate didn't look very pleased, but Rose finally took possession of the table and sat facing the entry to the tearoom, so Maureen O'Malley would be able to spot her easily.

"Nice work," her mother said through the leaves. She sounded as if she was talking out of the corner of her mouth.

"I'm ignoring you," Rose replied, barely moving her lips. "The hostess already thinks I have a screw loose. I won't let her catch me talking to the planter."

"The tea here isn't as good as I remembered."

"Ignoring you," Rose sang under her breath. Just then a stout woman in a green wool coat bustled into the tearoom and homed right in on Rose. Perched on her dyed red hair was a green derby with a feather in the band. Rose knew instantly that Maureen Fiona Keegan O'Malley had come upon the scene. As a kid, Rose had played around with ventriloquism, and she managed to smile and say "She's here" to her mother at the same time.

"Jesus, Mary and Joseph." Her mother sounded totally freaked out.

Maureen brushed the hostess aside and made straight for Rose's table. "If you aren't lovelier than your picture," she crooned. "Would you mind taking the other chair? The light's so much better over there and I want to get a really good look at you."

"It's a trick," whispered Bridget through the dieffenbachia.

Maureen looked startled. "Did you say something, Rose?"

"Just a little sneeze." Rose faked one and tried to make it sound like a whisper as she got up to trade chairs with Maureen.

"Must be my hearing. My Daniel told me to get it checked, but I've been putting it off, I have." Maureen took off her coat and draped it over the back of her chair before sitting down. She wore black stretch pants and an oversize flowered tunic containing every color in the rainbow.

"Daniel's your husband?" Rose asked, knowing her mother wanted every little detail. Personally, Rose was captivated by this sweet woman. Far from being "sheepfaced," she had expressive blue eyes and a wonderfully kind expression. Rose was beginning to feel guilty about the subterfuge.

"No, my husband was Patrick, bless his soul. Died in the line of duty, he did, two years ago in June."

"I'm sorry." A lonely widow. Rose felt worse and worse.

"Aye, 'twas a black day for sure, but at least I have Daniel, and he's a great comfort to me. Daniel's my son."

"I see." A slight uneasiness replaced Rose's goodwill.

"And speak of the devil, there he is, coming through the door!" Maureen waved enthusiastically.

Trapped. All Rose's kindly thoughts about Maureen O'Malley vanished.

"Come on over here, Daniel, my boy," said Maureen. "I have someone I want you to meet."

Rose closed her eyes in dismay.

Through the dieffenbachia came her mother's terse whisper: "Told you."

2

ROSE FELT the movement of air as Daniel paused right behind her.

"I can't believe this, Mom," he said in a deep baritone. "You've gone too far this time."

The voice was intriguing enough that Rose turned to face Maureen's son, although she thoroughly expected some nerdy guy who had to depend on his mother to arrange his dates.

Wrong. Daniel O'Malley towered above her, six feet of magnificent Irish manhood. With his leather jacket unzipped and his hands propped on his hips, he gave Rose an up-close-and-personal view of a tantalizingly broad chest tapering to a narrow waist. The wind had tousled his dark hair, making him look rumpled and sexy. All he needed was a passionate gaze to complete the picture. Although his deep brown eyes looked capable of melting the heart of any woman, they were currently snapping with anger as he confronted his mother.

Maureen seemed unfazed by his attitude. "Daniel O'Malley, where are your manners? Please say hello to Rose Kingsford. As I suspected, she's Irish. Gets it from her mother's side."

Rose heard violent coughing through the dieffenbachia. She ignored it, and held out her hand to this Celtic god. "Glad to meet you." A truer statement she'd never made.

Daniel's gaze moved down to connect with hers and his

angry stare gave way to a flush of embarrassment. "I apologize for the inconvenience," he said, his hand closing over hers. "I—I can't remember ever being so uncomfortable in my life."

"Don't give it another thought." Rose looked into his eyes as she returned the firm pressure of his handshake. The moment was brief, because he soon released her hand and concentrated on his mother again, but Rose reacted as if he'd suddenly swept her into his arms. Her heart was beating at a furious pace and she struggled for breath, but the turmoil within her made perfect sense. After all, she'd just met the man she would ask to father her child.

A waitress came up, gave Daniel an admiring glance and inquired if she should set another place at the table.

"Yes," Maureen said.

"No, that won't be necessary," Daniel said. "I'm not staying."

Rose had expected that and wasn't perturbed. She still had the mother in tow, and the mother wanted to match-make.

"Daniel, for heaven's sake," Maureen protested. "You can sit down and have a cup of tea, at least."

"I'm afraid not," he said with a quiet authority that prompted the waitress to retreat and tend to another customer. Then he turned toward Rose. "But it was nice meeting you." With that, he left the tearoom.

"Daniel!" Maureen called, but she might as well have saved the effort. He didn't even break stride. "Well, I guess I know what that's all about," Maureen said, glancing back at Rose. "His scar has made him dreadfully shy with the ladies."

"Scar?" Rose searched the vivid picture she now carried of Maureen's son. "I didn't notice any scar."

"That's because 'tis in a very...delicate spot, you see."

"Oh?" Rose could hear muffled noises coming from the other side of the planter where her mother was undoubtedly struggling to contain herself.

"'Tis on his, er, on his bum. Bullet wound."

"*Bullet* wound?"

"Well, naturally. He's a police officer with the mounted unit. Many of the lads he works with have been shot, one time or another. My Patrick had three bullet wounds. Got them before we were married, fortunately. The saints be praised he made detective right after we got married, so the work wasn't so dangerous."

"But didn't you say he died in the line of duty?"

Maureen nodded. "And so he did. Keeled over while he was at his desk making out a report. Fell face down into a box of donuts. Raised glazed."

The waitress's return saved Rose from trying to come up with a response to that detailed revelation. She decided to stick with just tea, but Maureen ordered a basket of muffins.

"You can share the muffins," Maureen said after the waitress left. "You could use a little more weight on your bones. Not that you aren't perfectly lovely the way you are. I know models are supposed to stay very thin. My best friend Bridget, the one you look so much like, was thin, too. She thought to go into modeling. 'Twas before she came to such a tragic end, you see."

The entire teapot on the other side of the planter hit the floor, judging from the splintering crash. The waitress hurried over and Rose pretended to cough into her napkin.

"Goodness, but that woman seems to be having a terrible lot of trouble over there," Maureen commented as she attempted to peer through the green barricade to the table next to them.

"Don't look," Rose cautioned, her voice low and

choked with laughter. "I saw her when I came in, and she's...not right, if you know what I mean. I'm sure we'd embarrass her by commenting on her struggles."

"Oh, dear." Maureen glanced away from the planter immediately. "Poor soul. Trying to get herself a little cheer, I expect. I'm surprised the tearoom let her in."

"They probably won't let her come back after this episode," Rose said. "Ah, here's our order."

After the waitress left them a steaming pot of tea and a basket of fragrant muffins, Rose settled in to gather information. "Tell me more about your son, Daniel."

"Well, he's not usually so abrupt, I promise you. Unless he's dealing with the criminal element, of course. He and his da were the same when it came to keeping the peace. The uniform seems to give him a harder edge, somehow."

"Interesting." Rose found the concept sexy.

"You should have seen him as a wee lad. Loved to run through the house buck naked."

"Really?" Rose figured Daniel would die a thousand deaths if he knew what stories his mother was telling about him.

"And smart as a whip." Maureen's blue eyes shone. "The sisters said he could be anything he wanted, but he chose police work, like his father. 'Tis a long-standing O'Malley tradition."

Intelligence, Rose thought, was very important for the purpose she had in mind. "Sisters? You have daughters?"

"No, the nuns, where he went to school. He played pranks, like most lads, but the sisters said 'twas probably because he got bored and needed to amuse himself." Maureen became incandescent with pride. "He ranked first in his class at the police academy."

"Remarkable." Rose moved to the next item on her mental list. "You have to be in pretty good shape to get on the police force, don't you?'' The table on the other side of the planter had become totally silent, and Rose could almost hear her mother listening to every syllable. Bridget was no dummy. She'd figured out why her daughter was taking this tack with Maureen. And she hated it.

"Indeed, you must be in good shape to get on the force,'' Maureen said. "But 'tis no problem for my Daniel. He inherited my good eyesight and he can do those push-ups like nobody's business. He's in grand condition.''

I would say so, Rose thought with admiration.

A warning hiss of breath came from beyond the leaves.

"Daniel is everything I would want in a son, except for one thing,'' Maureen said.

Rose set down her teacup and waited to hear the worst. Some inherited family disease, perhaps. Or maybe Daniel was gay and Maureen hoped Rose could turn him around.

The words came out in a rush. "He's thirty-three, and I say 'tis high time for him to settle down with some nice girl, but he says he won't do that until he makes detective, like my Patrick did, and when I ask him when that will be, he says not while he's having such a grand time riding with the mounted patrol unit.'' Maureen heaved a sigh and took a large bite of a muffin.

The litany sounded familiar to Rose. Her own mother's lectures ran along similar lines, except that Rose hadn't held out any hope to her mother about a day in the future when she'd get married. She just couldn't see the likelihood of it.

"'Tis the scar,'' Maureen said, regarding Rose with a hopeful expression. "Some lass needs to teach him not to be self-conscious about it. That would do the trick.''

Rose doubted the scar had anything to do with Daniel being marriage-shy. He probably just wasn't ready to settle down, which made him a perfect candidate for her plan.

But Maureen deserved a measure of honesty. "If you're looking for someone with marriage on her mind, I'm the wrong person, Mrs. O'Malley."

"You don't fancy Daniel?"

"I didn't say that. I'm just not interested in marriage."

"Then you *do* fancy him!"

"My goodness, what woman in her right mind wouldn't, Mrs. O'Malley?"

Maureen smiled with motherly satisfaction. "Lovely. That's a start." Pulling a stubby pencil and a scrap of paper from her purse, she scribbled on it and shoved it across the table toward Rose. "'Tis his phone number, if you'd like to call him. I'm willing to take my chances on the rest."

"Thank you. I will call him."

The groan through the dieffenbachia was barely muffled, as if Rose's mother was truly beside herself and no longer cared about detection.

Maureen shot a glance at the planter before leaning closer to Rose. "Should we do something? She sounds as if she's in mortal pain, she does. We could—"

"No, I don't think we should do anything," Rose said quickly. The last thing she wanted was for Maureen to discover Bridget and ruin everything. "From what I've read on the subject, you will only make them worse if you comment on their mental state."

"I think I'll just visit the Ladies, then, and take a look at her on the way, just to make sure she's not foaming at the mouth."

Figuratively, she probably was, Rose thought. "Just take care not to disturb her further," she cautioned Maureen.

"Right."

Rose held her breath as Maureen made her way through

the tearoom, but there was no surprised exclamation of recognition. The secret was safe for another few minutes.

"I know what you're up to!" Bridget said in a stage whisper. "Don't think I don't, Rose Erin Kingsford!"

Rose spoke in an undertone. "Mom, what's wrong with me wanting to go out with someone as cute as Daniel? Did you see him?"

"I saw him, all right. And you looking him up and down, like a mouse eyeing a wheel of cheese. And those questions you were asking, like he was on the auction block."

"He probably won't even go out with me after this incident with his mother."

"I have half a mind to reveal myself to Maureen. That would put the brakes on your little scheme, now, wouldn't it?"

Rose decided to call her bluff. "Go ahead. So I won't get a date with a cute guy. So what else is new?"

"I should. I really should. Here she comes, back from the Ladies."

"Then you have your chance, don't you?"

"Mutton dressed as lamb," Bridget muttered.

Rose braced herself, but nothing happened.

Maureen sat down again and leaned toward Rose before pointing toward the planter. "I've figured out her problem," she whispered. "You know that old movie *Breakfast at Tiffany's?*"

Rose nodded.

"That poor woman over there, who must be my age if she's a day, thinks she's playing the part in that picture. She thinks she's Audrey Hepburn."

Rose bit her lip to keep from laughing. Her mother wouldn't reveal herself in a million years after a remark like that. Maybe, just maybe, the date with Daniel O'Malley wasn't out of the question, after all.

UNLIKE HIS MOTHER, Daniel believed in answering machines. The next day when he arrived at his apartment after his shift, the message light on his answering machine was blinking, and he had a very good idea why. His mother had already told him that Rose Kingsford planned to call. They'd had quite a row about it, in fact. He winced as he remembered telling his own dear mother in no uncertain terms to get the hell out of his love life.

She'd promised to do that, but it was like closing the barn door after the horse escaped.

After changing into jeans and a sweatshirt, he made himself a corned-beef sandwich and opened a beer. He switched on the news and began to eat, all the while keeping an eye on that blinking red light and trying to imagine why Rose Kingsford was bothering with him. According to his mother, Rose "fancied" him, but then he didn't put much stock in anything his mother said about Rose.

He still couldn't believe that his mother had tracked down the model in the picture frame, arranged a meeting and then lured him there by pretending she wanted to have a cozy teatime chat, mother-and-son. Daniel hadn't realized how much of a rein his father must have kept on his mother. She would never have tried such a stunt while Patrick O'Malley was around. But lately she was acting like some...some *teenager*.

Finishing his sandwich and beer, Daniel wandered over to the living-room window of his small flat and stared out at the evening traffic below him. Moments such as this were somewhat lonely, but he was willing to pay that price. The first time he'd had to notify an officer's wife of the death of her husband, he'd vowed to do everything he could to avoid putting a woman through that. In a couple of years he'd seriously pursue a promotion that would take him out of the line of fire, and then maybe he'd consider finding a wife. On his own, without his mother's interference.

Her subdued reaction to his tirade told him she'd finally understood the line she must not cross again. But she'd left a loose end dangling, and he might as well deal with it now.

Turning from the window, he walked over to the answering machine and pushed the playback button. Rose Kingsford's voice came dancing from the speaker, with a lilt he would have recognized as hers even without her first identifying statement.

"Hi, Daniel. This is Rose Kingsford."

Rose Kingsford. Rose—a perfect name for a woman with laughing eyes, an upturned nose, a dusting of freckles, fiery hair and a smile that could swell a man's heart or rip it to shreds. Amazing how indelibly her image remained in his mind after more than twenty-four hours, when he'd only seen her for a few moments. Two armed robberies, an attempted rape and a four-car pileup should have erased the face of Rose Kingsford from his memory. But he could close his eyes and she was right in front of him, her hand so soft and delicate as she placed it in his....

"We got off to rather an unfortunate start. Perhaps if we met for dinner, we could repair the damage. I'm free on Tuesday night at seven." Then she named a little Italian restaurant in the Village.

Tuesday night was his first night off next week, and he was particularly fond of good Italian food—pieces of information his mother must have passed on. But the idea of Rose and his mother conspiring to rob him of his bachelor status just didn't make sense. Daniel had asked a cou-

ple of people today, and the consensus seemed to be that
a successful model pulled down at least a hundred grand
a year, most likely more. Somebody who looked like Rose
and made that kind of money wouldn't be interested in the
matchmaking schemes of some little Irish woman from
Brooklyn.

So what did Rose want of Daniel O'Malley? Or worse
yet, what outrageous stories had his mother told that had
convinced Rose to take pity on him and invite him to dinner? He could let the whole thing go, of course, and leave
the questions unanswered.

Like hell he could.

IN A SECLUDED BOOTH on a rainy Tuesday night Rose
watched the flame flicker in the small oil lamp centered
on the checkered tablecloth. Her stomach was in knots,
although she'd certainly asked men out on dates before.
After all, this was the nineties, and she wasn't the sort of
shrinking violet who hung back and waited for some man
to make the first move. But this was different. The out-
come of this meeting could change her entire life.

She'd decided that no man would react well to a frank
statement that she considered him the perfect candidate to
father her child. Some men might be flattered, but they
wouldn't be the type she'd want. Others would be pleased
at the idea of a one-night stand, but she also didn't want
that kind. She didn't think Daniel fit in either category.
Therefore, she'd have to handle the matter with great del-
icacy.

The timing couldn't have been better. Renovations were
complete on her little cottage upstate, and two rural New
York papers had agreed to carry her comic strip, "St.
Paddy and Flynn." She figured she was less than a year
from ending her modeling career and working full-time on

the strip, less than a year from settling into the country life she'd yearned for nearly all her life, it seemed. Pregnancy would push her into the decision to turn down future modeling jobs, and she would welcome the shove.

Of course Daniel might not show up tonight. She'd left the invitation on his answering machine without requiring an R.S.V.P. It was a calculated risk, but one that gave him the kind of leeway she'd thought necessary. It was the sort of gesture she'd have appreciated, in his shoes.

She glanced at her watch. Five minutes past seven. Her stomach lurched at the thought that he really might not come. Somehow her instincts had told her he would. She caught the eye of a waiter and ordered a glass of Chianti.

By seven-thirty she'd finished the wine, even though she'd sipped it very slowly. On an empty stomach, it had made her light-headed. And more than a little irritated. Sure, she hadn't forced him to respond to her invitation, but if he really hadn't meant to show he might have had the courtesy to notify her. Maybe a man who looked like Daniel had so many invitations he could afford to stand up several women a week. Maybe her precious instincts had been off somewhere napping when Daniel had arrived on the scene and simple lust had blinded her to his arrogant nature.

Well, she was sick of the pitying looks she kept getting from the waiter, who'd stopped by several times to inquire about whether she'd like to go ahead and order a meal. She was sick of sitting here waiting for some fellow who was so full of himself he took women's dinner invitations for granted. She was, finally and completely, sick of men in general. Maybe a sperm bank was the answer, after all.

Leaving money on the table for her wine and the time she'd spent in the booth, she gathered her trench coat and purse from the seat beside her. After shoving her arms angrily into the sleeves, she pushed her way out the restaurant door into the rain, where she started searching for a cab. Every one that sailed past her was occupied.

"Perfect. Just perfect," she muttered.

"Rose!"

When she heard her name, her heartbeat clicked into high gear. She turned and saw Daniel running toward her, his feet splashing through puddles in total abandon, as if he cared nothing for getting soaked so long as he reached her before she left. Instantly her anger evaporated, but she thought it prudent to retain some show of indignation.

"Rose, I'm so sorry." His breath came out in great clouds as he loped up beside her. "The cab got in a wreck about four blocks from here. Tourists in a Ford Tempo ran into him. Then when they discovered I was a cop...well, I had a devil of a time getting out of there." He paused. "I suppose you've eaten and are ready to go home."

She'd meant to chastise him for making her wait, but she was mesmerized with the way raindrops clung to his dark lashes. Then he blinked and one drop shook loose to run down the side of his nose and over to the corner of his mouth. She reached up and brushed it away. Then she glanced up into his eyes. There was the look she'd wished for when she'd seen him in the tearoom, the look that could melt a woman's heart.

Gently he pushed a damp tendril from her cheek and tucked it behind her ear. "You're getting wet."

"So are you."

His gaze caressed her face as he slid his hand over the nape of her neck. "It's only rain."

Her pulse pounded in her ears as she recognized the touch of a man who understood how to arouse a woman. What he was about to do was audacious, and all the more thrilling because of that. "I guess you're used to...the elements," she said.

"I'll tell you something, Rose." He leaned closer, his brown eyes warm with intent. "The elements never looked quite like this." Then, as the rain pattered all around them, he kissed her.

3

IN FOR A PENNY, in for a pound, Daniel thought as he took possession of Rose's moist, completely irresistible mouth. As a fact-finding mission, it wasn't a bad move. As he explored her velvet lips he learned several things—she tasted of honey and wine, she had the most responsive mouth he'd ever been fortunate enough to kiss, and he was trembling like a sapling in the wind from the excitement they generated together.

He had no idea how long he might have stood there enjoying the heated pleasure of kissing Rose, indifferent to the drizzle falling steadily on them, if a car hadn't whizzed through a puddle in the street beside them. The water hit them with enough velocity to awaken them from their daze. They broke apart and stared at each other in shock, as though just now realizing what had happened between them.

Rose started laughing first, and the sound filled the rain-soaked air with such delight that before Daniel realized it, he was laughing, too. His shoes, relatively new, were ruined, and God knew if he'd ever get the mud stains out of his slacks. He didn't care.

"Let's go inside and get some pasta," she said.

"And more of that wine."

"Wine?"

"I could taste it."

"Oh." Her cheeks grew even pinker.

A maidenly blush. He was enchanted out of his mind. He took her elbow and propelled her toward the restaurant to keep himself from making an indecent proposal and luring her back to his flat this very minute. He still didn't know what Rose Kingsford wanted with him, but he was getting some idea of what he wanted with her.

The restaurant was almost deserted as they dripped their way back to a booth. A teenaged boy appeared from the kitchen to follow them with a rag mop, and Daniel turned and gave him a tip. Then he took off his jacket and handed it to the waiter who appeared at their table. He suggested Rose do the same. "Can you find a place to hang these where they can dry?" he asked the waiter.

"Sure thing."

"And bring a bottle of wine, the same kind she had before."

"You couldn't tell what kind it was?" Rose teased as the waiter left.

"It was Chianti, but I didn't want to show off." Then he adjusted the little oil lamp so he could look at her. He had a feeling the activity could absorb his attention for some time.

She leaned her chin on her fist and seemed to be copying his behavior. "So you decided to come, after all."

"Can't resist a good Italian meal, but then I guess you know that."

She smiled.

He pretended to shield his eyes from the brilliance. "You know, you should have that thing registered. Could cause blindness."

Her smile broadened into a chuckle.

He grinned back, inordinately pleased with himself. Even though he knew rationally that she smiled for a living, he decided he would kid himself that this one had been for him and him alone. "Besides my fondness for Italian food and what nights I'm off duty, what did my mother tell you about me?"

A secret sparkle lurked in her green eyes.

"Come on, let's have it."

"Am I being interrogated?"

"You bet your sweet shamrocks. No telling what that woman's been spreading around town in hopes of getting me to the altar." He regarded her intently and took a deep breath. Honesty was called for. "In spite of what just happened outside, I'm not in the market for a wife, Rose."

"She told me that."

"No doubt she had some twisted version of why that is."

She remained silent, but the dancing light in her eyes told him that Maureen had indeed made up some woolly tale that explained his single status.

"Whatever it is, it's not true," he said. "I'm single because that's what I choose to be right now."

"Same here."

He fell backward against the booth in feigned shock. "What? No arguments about the blissful wedded state?"

"I have no interest in getting married, either."

"Does my sainted mother know this singular fact about you?"

"I told her. She gave me your phone number and said she'd take her chances."

Daniel considered this as the bottle of Chianti arrived and they both ordered dinner. After the waiter left, Daniel sipped his wine until their sense of intimacy had reasserted itself. Then he leaned both arms on the table and fixed Rose with a steady gaze. "So you don't want a husband."

"No. Have no interest in that, thank you."

"Then what do you want, Rose Kingsford?" He

watched her eyes and knew before she opened her mouth that he wasn't about to get the whole truth. Twelve years in police work had taught him that much.

"Believe it or not, I find it difficult to meet men," she began.

"I don't believe it."

"Well, it's true." She took a long, graceful sip of her wine. "First, there are the male models. Chuck, the best of that bunch, is gay. Then there are the photographers. Some are great, usually the married ones, and some are sleazeballs—grope city."

"Sounds unpleasant."

Rose sighed. "I don't know if it's just the nature of what I do, putting my body out there for everyone to see, but most men seem to be focused on that body and not the person, which turns me off. Besides that, I work very hard and put in a lot of hours. When I have time off I don't feel like making the effort to hit the nightclubs, so the result is…not much chance to meet regular guys."

"That's how you'd classify me?"

"I'd classify you as the deluxe model."

He nearly choked on his wine. "Isn't that a little extravagant, considering we've known each other less than an hour?"

"I trust my instincts. In your line of work, I'm sure you do, too."

"That's why I'm here." *And why I kissed you.*

She gazed at him over the rim of her goblet. "Do you know how many men concentrate on my eyes when we meet?"

"I have no idea."

"Almost none. But you did."

"I was embarrassed. I don't know if you can give me much credit for the way I behaved, considering that my mother had just put me in one of the most awkward situations any man can imagine. Maybe if we'd met at a cocktail party I'd have given you the full-body once-over, like all the others.''

"I don't think so, Daniel O'Malley." She turned on that million-dollar smile again. "I don't think so at all."

"Talk about hamstringing a guy. I'm going to be afraid to look below the level of your nose from now on, for fear you'll bump my classification down to sleazeball, fourth class."

"Wrong. You passed the test, so you can relax."

"Hey, that's great. Would you mind standing up, then?"

She blinked. "Excuse me?"

He stifled a grin and motioned her up. "Ogling time. I figure I'm behind on my quota."

She gazed at him for a full thirty seconds and he figured that was the end of that. She couldn't take a joke, and it was good that he'd found it out now before things progressed beyond that sizzling kiss.

Then she slowly eased out of the booth. "Pay attention," she said. "I only intend to do this once." She stood and smoothed her damp clothes, a leather miniskirt, knee-high boots, a form-fitting knit top and a funky little vest with tiny gold chains all over it. Lifting her chin and squaring her shoulders, she threw him a look of haughty confidence before moving sinuously down the aisle beside the booths.

Daniel realized she'd mentally placed herself on a runway. In total awe, he sank back against the booth and watched the provocative sway of her slender hips as she walked away from him on those terrific legs. No wonder guys skipped looking into her eyes, he thought. The message coming from the rest of her was too potent for mere mortals to ignore.

Just before she reached the kitchen door she pivoted and started back. Her breasts were small, but she thrust them forward so seductively that Daniel's mouth went dry as the little chains on her vest danced invitingly. Thank God he had a table to cover the effect she was having on him. Usually attracted to more well-endowed women, he would never have imagined someone as willowy as Rose would inspire such lust. Carriage was everything, apparently, and Rose had that in spades.

He decided to concentrate on her face to keep himself from starting to drool. No help there. She'd turned the heat up from warm and sweet to hot and smoldering. He took a deep breath and gripped the table as she drew nearer. It was either that or throw her down on top of it once she came close enough.

She reached their table and glanced down at him as if he were one of her subjects. Which he was, now. She had only to command him.

"Well?" she asked.

He cleared his throat. "Thanks," he managed.

She slid into the booth and the arrogance slipped from her like a cloak. "Now we're even."

He didn't think they were on the same playing field, let alone even. "What do you mean?"

"I've been watching you for days."

"What?"

"As luck would have it, I was working this past week quite close to your…beat, I guess you call it. I'm a sucker for a guy in a uniform, and then, when you climb up on that magnificent horse…" The corners of her mouth twitched in amusement. "Let's just say I did my share of ogling, too."

Heat crept up from his damp collar. "I didn't see you."

"I was using binoculars."

"Good grief."

She chuckled. "I've embarrassed you. But that's a good sign. You're not vain, at any rate."

Daniel was speechless. When the waiter showed up with their dinner he'd never been so glad to see a plate of pasta in his life. "Thank God. I'm starved," he said. As he picked up his fork he glanced at Rose and caught her smiling at him. "Binoculars? Really?"

"Don't sound so surprised. You cut quite a figure, as my mother would say."

"Your Irish mother," he said, remembering his own mother's comment that afternoon in the tearoom. "Where's she from?"

"Tralee."

He finished a bite of the most succulent linguine he'd ever tasted. He liked Rose's choice in restaurants, among other things. "That's quite a coincidence, considering that my mother comes from Tralee. You don't suppose that they knew each—"

"I'm sure not," she said quickly.

Too quickly, he thought. The plot was thickening. "Does your mother live in New York?"

"Oh, yes."

There was a world of meaning in that phrase, he thought. "Sounds like your mother's somewhat of a trial to you, too."

"Let's just say we don't agree on how I should live my life."

"Let me guess. She'd like you to find some nice guy and settle down."

Rose paused with a forkful of fettucine halfway to her mouth. "Bingo."

"And your father?"

"He doesn't get much say in the matter. They're divorced."

"His idea?"

She took a long swallow of Chianti. "Yep."

That could explain her aversion to marriage, he thought, and decided to risk finding out. "Look, I don't really know you well enough to ask this—"

"Yes, you do." She met his gaze across the subtle flame of the oil lamp.

Those green eyes. He was helpless, going down for the count. Green was supposed to be a cool color, but there was nothing even remotely cool about the way she was looking at him.

"What did you want to ask?" she murmured.

He hadn't the slightest idea. More important questions had begun to shove out whatever inane thing he'd been about to say. Questions that began with *when* and *where*. Then his pager vibrated against his thigh. He extracted it from his pocket and reluctantly broke eye contact with Rose in order to check the number. Damn. The station.

"I have to make a quick phone call," he said. "Be right back."

"That would be nice."

He slid from the booth with a silent prayer that this wasn't a call asking him to go in to work. The prayer went unanswered. On his way back from using the pay phone in the back of the restaurant he found the waiter and told him to bring the check and his jacket.

"Problems?" Rose asked as he returned to the booth.

"A guy called in sick. I have to leave, but I hope you'll stay and finish your meal."

"Don't worry. I will. Maybe yours, too." She glanced up as the waiter approached with the check and Daniel's jacket. She held out her hand to the waiter. "This one's on me."

The waiter started toward her.

"I'm afraid not." Daniel motioned for the check.

The waiter sighed and looked at the ceiling. "Oh, boy."

"Daniel, I invited you to dinner. It's as simple as that."

The waiter gritted his teeth and stepped toward her again.

Daniel interceded and took the bill from him. "No, it's even simpler. When I have dinner with a woman, I pay for it. End of discussion." He reached in his back pocket for his wallet.

"I won't let you do this."

"Let him," the waiter said.

"Yeah, let me." Daniel glanced at the total and pulled some bills from his wallet. "Thanks," he said to the waiter, putting both the check and money in the guy's hand. Then he shrugged into his jacket. "I'll call you," he said as he started out of the restaurant.

"That's what they all say," the waiter commented to Rose.

Daniel turned and backed toward the door as he zipped his jacket. "In this case, it happens to be true." Then he gave Rose a salute and went outside to look for a cab. The rain had stopped, but a chill wind had picked up. Daniel had just whistled a cab over when Rose came out of the restaurant, coatless.

"Daniel, I'm paying for dinner!" she said, shoving the money at him.

"No, you're not." He took her by the shoulders and turned her around. "Now go back inside. It's cold out here."

"You want a cab or not?" the cabbie called from the window.

"Yeah," Daniel said over his shoulder.

"Meter's running, then."

"Come on, Daniel." She twisted in his grip. "Don't be so old-fashioned."

"But you see, that's exactly what I am." He turned her to face him again. "Look, I know you could buy and sell me. Let me preserve some of my pride by taking care of dinner."

She gazed at him. "I don't care how much money you make or don't make. That's not the point."

"It is for me."

She closed her eyes in apparent frustration. "You know, I really—"

He interrupted her protest by pulling her close.

Her eyes flew open.

"Forgot something," he murmured. "Dessert." Then he gave himself up to the richness of her mouth. Oh, the promise of those ripe lips. He cursed Tom Peterson, who had had the poor judgment to call in sick tonight. Otherwise, this evening might have ended quite differently.

The cabbie beeped the horn and Daniel lifted his head with regret. "Gotta go."

Rose's lashes drifted upward and she reached to stroke his cheek with the tip of her finger. "I'll accept your generosity tonight on one condition."

"What's that?"

"Next time, I'll cook."

It took only a fraction of a second for the implication of that to sink in, and his body tightened in anticipation. "All right."

She eased out of his embrace. "Next Tuesday, same time?"

"You've got it."

She backed toward the restaurant. "I'll leave my address on your machine."

"Fine."

"Good night, Daniel."

"Good night." He remained standing there long after the door closed behind her.

The cab window creaked down again. "It's your business, buddy, but holding down the sidewalk is getting pretty expensive, don't you think?"

Daniel turned and climbed into the cab.

"However—" The cabbie pronounced it "howevah." "I completely understand being distracted with a woman who looks like that."

MAUREEN DIDN'T ABUSE the privilege of having a key to her son's apartment. He'd given it to her for the times she came into Manhattan from Brooklyn to shop and wanted someplace to freshen up, someplace she could trust would be clean and safe.

Maureen never snooped through Daniel's dresser drawers or his mail. Daniel always laughed and told her to go ahead. There weren't any secrets in his apartment. Up until now she'd believed him, but in the past week he'd become more secretive. 'Twas pure luck that she discovered why.

She'd taken the subway into the city for a sale at Macy's and stopped at Daniel's afterward, as usual. While she was making herself a restorative cup of tea, Daniel's telephone rang. She hurried to pick up the receiver, but just then Daniel's voice came on and she remembered about the answering machine. The contraption confused her something awful, and she wasn't about to fool with it.

Instead she stood there and listened to Daniel's brisk message. He sounded so businesslike on that recording that whenever she got the machine she just hung up. Probably this person would, too. Daniel's social life would pick up considerably if he got rid of this machine, in Maureen's humble opinion.

But the person on the other end didn't hang up. Instead, Maureen listened in wonder as Rose Kingsford gave Daniel directions to her apartment and reminded him that they'd settled on Tuesday at seven. Maureen clapped a hand over her mouth as if afraid that Rose could hear her giggle of delight. Dinner at Rose's apartment! That little devil Daniel had never let on that matters had progressed to this stage. If a woman cooked a man dinner, then she meant to demonstrate her domestic skills for him.

After Rose hung up, Maureen picked up her skirts and danced a jig around the apartment. Oh, this was grand news! She'd had a feeling about this girl from the moment she'd laid eyes on her, and now, the romance was getting under way! The jig didn't last very long before she was out of breath, but as she plopped to the couch and put a hand over her beating heart, she continued to smile.

Then she bounced up again, hurried to the bookcase and found the street map. Digging in her purse for her reading glasses, Maureen located the spot where the apartment house must be. Rose lived in a swanky part of town, all right. Maureen would dearly love to see Daniel walk into that place. She wondered if he'd take flowers. 'Twould be a good sign, if he took flowers.

As closemouthed as Daniel had become lately, he probably wouldn't tell her whether he went over to Rose's, let alone whether he took flowers. Maureen picked up a pad of paper beside the phone and wrote down Rose's address. 'Twould be quite dark at seven. She'd take a cab, never mind the expense. The sight of Daniel walking into that apartment building with a bouquet of flowers would be a picture she'd carry to her grave. Her Daniel was going courting.

SOMETHING WAS GOING ON. Bridget Kingsford was sure of it. Tuesday was the night Rose always came over to watch their favorite television shows, unless she was out of town on a shoot. When she'd cancelled out for the second Tuesday in a row, and offered no explanation, Bridget feared it had something to do with Daniel O'Malley.

It was a long shot, but maybe if she just dropped in on Rose Tuesday night, she'd find out something. A chat with the doorman might work almost as well. Bridget didn't intend to stand by while her daughter conceived a child out of wedlock, most especially if the prospective father was the son of her age-old rival. She'd sooner dance with the devil on the steps of St. Patrick's Cathedral than allow that to take place.

4

ROSE HAD FIGURED on learning to cook someday. For one thing, she couldn't imagine being a mother and not knowing how to bake chocolate chip cookies. It was one of her favorite fantasies of motherhood—a warm kitchen filled with the aroma of baking dough as a little child perched on a stool, her fat fingers making chip-filled balls and arranging them carefully on a cookie sheet.

Rose's mother had always made cooking seem easy enough, although her recent obsession with her figure had ended some of her enthusiasm for baking. Rose would have loved to ask for some motherly advice on the meal she planned to serve Daniel on Tuesday night. But her mother wasn't supposed to know about that meal, or any of the activities that might follow.

As luck would have it, the Donna Karan shoot on Tuesday afternoon had run overtime, which had screwed up her cooking schedule and stressed her out. That probably explained why she'd cut her finger trying to machete some celery stalks into submission while keeping one eye on the clock. She stuck her finger in her mouth and ran for the bathroom cabinet where she hoped at least one bandage remained in the box she kept there.

Daniel was scheduled to arrive in forty minutes. According to the recipe, the stew needed nearly two hours to cook, and she had yet to brown the meat. Thank God she'd bought a decent bottle of cabernet to fill the extra hour the stew would require to cook. That was assuming she got everything in the pot within the next five minutes.

The bandage box was empty, so she fastened a tissue around her bleeding finger with masking tape from her drafting supplies and headed back to the kitchen. Ten minutes later, her knit top and jeans were coated in flour from rolling the cubed lamb in it, her forearm was taped with more tissue where hot grease had splattered while she browned the meat, and her eyes watered madly from chopping an onion. When she wiped her streaming eyes with the back of her hands, she got flour all over her face, too.

"Jesus, Mary and Joseph," she muttered, using one of her mother's favorite angry expressions. She finished chopping the onion and sighed. If she could get the stew in the oven, then shower and change, she'd decant the wine before Daniel arrived. With wine and intimate conversation, perhaps he'd never notice that dinner was delayed. She continued reading the recipe aloud.

"Tie parsley, celery, bay leaves and thyme in small bag," she murmured. *A small bag?* It made no sense. She had a couple of small paper bags, but they'd disintegrate in the stew. A plastic bag would melt. She left the kitchen and roamed the apartment, seeking inspiration. Twice she reached for the phone to call her mother before remembering she couldn't do that.

Finally she wandered into her bedroom where a dresser drawer hung open, its contents spilling out from her rush to find clean underwear that morning. A nylon stocking dangled nearly to the floor.

She pounced on the drawer as she remembered getting a run in a pair of Dark Seduction panty hose just yesterday. They had little spangles all over them, but so what? The stew wouldn't know the difference if the spices were encased in spangles or not. Moments later she'd amputated the foot from the panty hose. She washed and rinsed the bit of nylon, dumped the spices in the toe, knotted the ankle, and plopped the whole thing into the stew.

"Cook fast," she instructed the stew as she slid it into the oven and glanced at the clock. She twisted the oven dial up a few extra notches, figuring a higher temperature would make the stew cook faster.

She had nine minutes to make herself presentable. As she hurried toward her bedroom, the intercom buzzed. She walked to the intercom with a feeling of inevitability and pushed the button. "Yes?"

"Daniel O'Malley's here to see you," said Jimmy, who monitored the desk in the lobby most evenings. "Shall I send him up?"

Rose glanced down at her flour-covered clothes, then touched a flour-covered hand to her tangle of hair caught up in a clip. She'd need at least fifteen minutes to transform herself. Daniel was a good eight minutes early, but if she made him wait downstairs, he'd think he had a vain woman on his hands. Considering her career choice, she already had to fight that image with most people, and she didn't want to fight it with Daniel. For all she knew, he'd arrived early as a sort of test.

"Sure, send him up," she said.

Then she raced for a pad of paper, scribbled a note that invited him to come in, and unlocked the door to tape it on the outside. *The wine*. She should have it uncorked and a goblet sitting beside the bottle on the coffee table so he could help himself while she showered and changed. That would be a classy gesture and show she had his comfort in mind even though he'd have to wait.

Dashing into the kitchen, she wrenched open the drawer where she usually kept the corkscrew—the drawer where she also kept the scissors, the coupons for microwave dinners, the corks she saved from memorable wine tastings with friends, the dried remnants of a rose her mother had given her on her last birthday, toothpicks, and matches from every restaurant she'd ever been to in New York.

The corkscrew refused to show itself as she pawed through the jumbled contents of the drawer. Finally she glanced on the counter and saw the corkscrew lying where she'd left it for convenience, right next to the wine bottle. "Aha! Now I've got you, my pretty!"

She picked up the knife she'd used to cut both the celery and her finger, pared away the seal and twisted the corkscrew in. Then she tugged, but the cork wouldn't budge.

"Open up, you son of a cheap jug wine!" She stuck the bottle between her legs for leverage and started to yank the cork out.

"You shouldn't leave your door unlocked."

Rose shrieked in alarm. Pulling out the cork at the same time as she yelled was pure reflex. Without Daniel diving to catch it, the bottle would have hit the floor. As it was, it merely disgorged a couple of ounces on his brown leather boots as the weight of the bottle crushed the bouquet of violets he held in one hand.

Rose grabbed a dishcloth from the sink and dropped to her knees in front of him. "Don't move!" she instructed as she dabbed at the wine staining the soft leather.

"Hey, don't bother. It's okay."

"This is nice leather. I don't want to ruin—" She forgot what she'd meant to say as he crouched down and set the wine bottle and mangled flowers on the floor.

"It's okay," he said again, taking her by her arms and drawing her gently to her feet.

"No, it's not." She imagined how she must look to him with flour all over her, including in her hair, and not a speck of makeup on. "In fact, the disasters that have happened in this kitchen recently make *Twister* look like a comedy.''

A smile flitted across his face, but his brown eyes were grave. ''If you leave your door unlocked again, things could get a whole lot worse.''

''I thought I'd be in the shower when you arrived.'' His firm grip on her arms was interfering with clear thinking. Old Spice. She'd forgotten he used it. No designer cologne for this guy. ''I'm...running a little late.''

''So you left a note on the door inviting me and any wacko who happened along to walk right in and make himself at home? Not good, Rose.''

She'd about come to the end of her tether. Nothing was turning out the way she'd planned, and now she was getting a lecture from the man she'd hoped to seduce. Tears threatened, but she blinked them back and lifted her chin in defiance. ''Gonna arrest me for gross negligence, officer?''

''I—hey, don't cry. Aw, hell.'' He pulled her into his arms, flour and all.

''Daniel, don't! I'm covered with—''

''So I noticed.'' His mouth came down on hers.

With the first pressure of his lips, her luck began to change. Whoever had coined the phrase ''kiss it and make it better'' must have had Daniel O'Malley in mind for the job. All her anxiety over the meal and her appearance dissolved before the tender onslaught of his mouth on hers. Tension slipped from her body until she felt as liquid as the wine in the bottle she'd been trying to open.

He ended the kiss slowly, with exquisite timing. She lifted suddenly heavy eyelids to gaze up at him.

''I'm sorry I barked at you,'' he murmured.

The belligerence had been kissed right out of her. ''I suppose you had a point about the unlocked door.''

"I did, but I could also see how much trouble you were taking to cook me a meal." He rubbed the flat of his hand up and down her spine in a caress that soothed, yet stimulated at the same time. "I could have mentioned that before delivering my standard cop safety lecture."

She let out a long sigh. "I'm not much of a cook, Daniel. My mother's a great cook. I should have learned more from her, but I just haven't taken the time."

The corners of his mouth turned up. "You sound as if you're in a confessional relating a string of murders. It's not a sin, you know."

"The way I was raised, it is. And the way you were raised, I'd imagine. You said you were an old-fashioned guy."

"If you mean that my mother's a traditional housewife, you'd be right. If you mean that I expect that role of all women, that I'm *that* kind of old-fashioned guy, you'd be wrong. I may be an Irish cop, but that's where the stereotype ends."

"But you insisted on paying for dinner."

He grinned. "Well, now, that's another whole issue. I had to establish my status."

"Status?"

"I don't want to be your boy toy."

"Oh, for heaven's sake! I would never—"

"Maybe not." He stopped rubbing her back and gazed at her intently. "But let's not kid ourselves that you're not one up on me in the fame-and-fortune department. I want it clearly understood from the beginning that I pay my own way. Don't invite me to St. Thomas for the weekend. I can't afford it."

She chuckled and leaned back in his arms. "You can relax on that score. I have no intention of inviting you to St. Thomas for the weekend."

"Oh."

He looked so deflated she took pity on him. "*I* don't go to St. Thomas for the weekend."

"Okay, so I got the destination wrong. I'm not sure what tropical vacation spots are trendy these days."

"I don't take tropical vacations. The only way I get to those places is if my job sends me there." She stepped out of his arms and took his hand. "Come on. I'll show you what I spend my free time and money on."

"If it's illegal, I don't want to know about it."

She laughed as she led him toward her office. "You have a very jaded view of what people do with big salaries, bucko."

"I'm a New York City cop."

"Well, you'll find nothing to confiscate here." At her office door she became nervous about watching him study the work spread on her drafting table. "Give me your jacket and I'll hang it up while you're searching the place."

As he shrugged out of his leather jacket and handed it to her, she took a moment to admire the way his knit Henley defined the muscled breadth of his chest. Her fingers itched to undo the buttons and explore what lay beneath. Talk about chemistry. Every move he made brought a flush of anticipation to her skin.

She waved her hand toward her office. "Go ahead. I'll be right back." The decision to show him her cartooning work had been made impulsively, but as she hung his jacket in the hall closet she decided it was the right decision. The more he understood about her, the more likely he'd be to grant her ultimate request. She was encouraged by his statement that he wasn't a stereotypical Irish male who expected women to conform to a certain standard.

After hanging up the jacket, she returned to her office

and paused in the doorway. Daniel stood in front of the drafting table, his back to her, his hands braced on his hips as he studied her cartoons. He chuckled, then laughed outright. She smiled with pleasure. Feeling far more confident than she had five minutes ago, she walked up beside him.

He glanced at her with a look of admiration. "These are great, Rose. Better than the ones in the *Times*."

"So far nobody at the *Times* agrees with you, but I've sold the strip to a couple of small papers upstate."

"No kidding? Congratulations." He returned his attention to the drafting table. "I don't have to ask you where you get your ideas. You've been listening in on a lot of Irish conversations."

"Then you think I have the tone right?"

"It's uncanny. St. Paddy sounds just like my dad, and the little leprechaun's comebacks are exactly what my mother used to say to him. If I didn't know better I'd think you'd been eavesdropping all these years."

"Well, my grandmother, who spent one summer with us, talked that way, and I was in Ireland last year while we photographed the shots for my calendar."

He looked at her. "Calendar? I don't remember seeing one."

"You keep up with calendars?"

"In the past week I've done a study of magazines and calendars. My version of your routine with the binoculars."

She lifted her eyebrows. "I see. Well, this one's in production for next year. I'm hoping the royalties on it will cushion the loss of income when I retire from modeling in the next year or so."

"Now I'm really intimidated. You've saved enough money to retire already?"

"Not retire the way you're thinking. But I can last a few years while I work on getting the strip going."

"Whew." He gazed at her and shook his head. "And here I thought you were a free spirit whose top priority was—" he paused "—a relationship."

"That isn't what you were about to say."

"What I was about to say was uncalled for."

She moved closer to him. "Maybe it was correct."

"I doubt it. A woman with your sort of self-direction is a hell of a lot deeper than I was going to give you credit for."

"That doesn't mean I don't have…needs."

"I'm sure you do. But you'd never let them get in the way of your master plan."

She allowed herself to become lost in the power of his dark eyes. "Is that so bad?"

"I can't say it is. I'm the same way."

The impulse to unfasten the first button on his shirt became too strong to resist. "Then I guess we have a perfect situation," she murmured.

"It seems that way." His voice had taken on a huskier tone.

She moved to the second button and her fingers brushed against a tendril of dark chest hair. Her breathing quickened.

"What about dinner?" he asked softly.

She undid another button and looked up at him. "Dinner will take a while longer to cook."

He slid a hand along her jawline and tipped her mouth up to his. "That's the best news I've heard all night."

MAUREEN HAD MEANT to watch from the cab as Daniel walked into the apartment-building lobby, and then take the cab back home. But once he'd disappeared from sight she couldn't seem to leave. All her dreams could be coming true in that apartment building, and she wanted to savor the moment. Taking the cab to this spot had been terribly expensive, but justified. Sitting there with the meter running was pure extravagance, however.

"Pull up in front of the apartment," she instructed the driver. "I'm getting out."

"You want me to wait for you?" the driver asked.

"No, thank you." She dug out the proper amount from her purse and added a tip before putting it in the money chute set into the sheet of plastic that divided the front and back seats. "I'll call another cab when I need one."

"Suit yourself."

Maureen climbed out onto the sidewalk. She'd just stand here a moment, she thought, looking up at the rows of lighted windows above her. If only she knew for certain that one of those lighted windows belonged to Rose Kingsford. But perhaps Rose didn't have an apartment that looked out on the street.

A cold raindrop hit her in the eye, and then another. She opened her purse and fished around until she found the accordian-folded rain bonnet she carried everywhere. She tied it securely over her hair and hoped the rain would let up.

It started coming down harder, pelting her plastic bonnet as if the good Lord had got it into his head to drown her on the spot. New York raindrops seemed to hit a body harder than Irish rain, Maureen thought. Or at least the way she remembered Irish rain. Someday she'd love to go back and find out if she remembered right.

Soon she was standing in a puddle. No help for it, she'd have to head into the apartment lobby.

She scurried through the revolving door and stood blinking in the brightness of the interior. But she certainly approved of the atmosphere. A crystal chandelier sparkled above her, and what looked like very fine paintings hung on the wallpapered walls. Two wing chairs in a burgundy-and-gray print sat on either side of a small table with a lovely flower arrangement on it. Maureen wondered if she dared sit in one of the chairs for a wee bit.

"Can I help you, ma'am?" asked a nice-looking young man from behind an antique desk that had a computer on it.

"I was…uh…meeting someone, I was." She untied her rain bonnet. "But I think she must have been held up. I needed a place to get in out of the weather, you see. What is your name, young man?"

"I'm Jimmy, ma'am. Would you like me to call a cab for you?"

Maureen thought about that. She did so hate to leave the scene, but parking herself in the lobby might get awkward. "I'll wait a little longer, Jimmy," she said. "And then, if she doesn't come, I would be most obliged if you would call for a cab."

Jimmy smiled. "All right."

Maureen decided to talk with Jimmy, which might keep him from thinking she was some sort of bag lady. She noticed a textbook lying open on the desk and walked over toward where he sat. "Looks like you're studying for something, Jimmy."

"Yep. Economics exam tomorrow."

"Economics. 'Tis a good field. My son Daniel decided to go to the police academy. He's with the mounted patrol."

Jimmy nodded. "That sounds—" He paused and glanced past her toward the door. "Why, hello there, Mrs. Kingsford."

"Hello, Jimmy," said a woman who had apparently just entered the lobby.

Mrs. Kingsford, Maureen thought with a thrill of excitement. It had to be Rose's mother, Daniel's future mother-in-law! The luck of the Irish was with Maureen tonight for sure. You could tell a lot about how a girl would turn out by looking at her mother, in Maureen's opinion, and here was a chance to find out about Rose's mother early on, without revealing that she was Daniel's mother. Putting on her best smile, Maureen turned.

The woman named Mrs. Kingsford stared at Maureen, and Maureen stared back. The poor demented bag lady from the tearoom!

A look of horror contorted the woman's face. "You!" she screamed.

5

DANIEL'S HEART galloped faster as Rose nestled her lithe body seductively close and opened her mouth beneath his. He'd never received such a delicious invitation in his life, and he was more than ready to accept it.

Holding Rose was like holding an arc of electricity. She galvanized every inch of him until he fairly hummed with the need to touch, to stroke, to possess her in the most intimate way possible. He didn't remember pulling her knit top from the waistband of her jeans, yet he must have, for soon his hands were gliding over warm, silken skin.

She wore nothing beneath the top, and the sweet weight of her breast filled his hand as if he'd been born to caress her this way. She trembled and gasped against his mouth, and fierce, almost frightening needs surged through him. He wondered if they'd make it into her bedroom or be forced by their driving passion to satisfy themselves on the floor of her office.

She kissed him as if she couldn't get enough, while her busy hands pulled his shirt out and lightly raked his back with her nails. As his breathing grew labored, his senses filled with her floral cologne and the intoxicating scent of thoroughly aroused woman.

He also smelled something burning.

He tried not to acknowledge it. Her lips tasted like heaven and he eagerly anticipated tasting the rest of her willing body. He didn't want something to be burning.

But it sure as hell was. Cursing the training that refused to let him ignore even the slightest hint of danger, he lifted his mouth from hers. "I think——" He stopped to clear the huskiness of desire from his throat. "There could be a problem in the kitchen."

She moaned softly.

He steeled himself not to return to lips blushing from his enthusiastic kisses. Reluctantly he removed his hand from her breast. "Rose, something's burning."

Her eyelids lifted, revealing green eyes sultry with desire.

One look into those eyes and he became as unconcerned as Nero when Rome was torched. "Never mind," he said as he lowered his head again.

Her nose wrinkled. "Something *is* burning!" She wiggled out of his embrace and rushed from the room.

He followed as best he could, considering his jeans had become way too tight in the past ten minutes.

Rose stood coughing in front of an open oven door, and the kitchen was enveloped in smoke. "It's our dinner!" she wailed, pulling on oven mitts before hauling out a smoking roaster and banging it onto the top of the stove. "It's ruined."

He took refuge in the timeworn male response to this sort of disaster. "We'll go out."

"I don't want to go out. I want to fix you a nice, home-cooked meal!" She lifted the roaster lid and more smoke billowed out. "Look at this! It's——it's——" She peered into the roaster and her eyes widened. "It's *sparkling*."

"Sparkling?" Daniel had witnessed a few kitchen disasters in his time, but none of them had sparkled. He stepped forward and surveyed the charred mess in the pan. Sure enough, sprinkled throughout the glop were tiny stars that winked in the kitchen's overhead light. He glanced at Rose in confusion.

"I'm not even going to tell you." She slammed the lid back on the roaster.

He chuckled and grabbed her by the arms. "What do you mean, you're not going to tell me? I deserve to know why there are stars in the stew."

She blushed and averted her gaze. "I doubt it would have affected the taste."

"What wouldn't?"

"My Dark Seduction panty hose."

He couldn't stop the laughter that rolled out. "You put panty hose in our dinner? Where'd you get the recipe, from an episode of 'The Addams Family'?"

She twisted out of his grip. "Go ahead and make fun of me. I told you I'm not a very good cook, but at least I tried."

He composed himself with difficulty. "I can see that. I apologize for laughing. But if you don't explain what the panty hose were doing in that stew, I'll go crazy trying to imagine what your reasoning was. Have some pity on me, Rose."

"You have to promise not to laugh if I tell you."

"I promise."

"I used the panty hose to hold the spices."

"The spices?" His lips twitched. "You must have used a bay leaf the size of a Buick."

"Daniel! You promised!"

"Right." He pressed his lips together and looked up at the ceiling. "I take it your panty hose had little stars on them."

"I didn't think they'd come *off.*"

"Of course not." He looked at her, his eyes brimming with the effort not to laugh. He'd never seen anything so cute in his life. Here was one of New York's top models, a talented cartoonist, an astute businesswoman, a passionate lover...and clueless in the kitchen. Yet she'd attempted to cook him what appeared to have once been an Irish stew. She flattered him more than she knew.

She took off her oven mitts and tossed them on the counter. "Well, I've certainly botched everything, haven't I?"

"Not at all." He closed the distance between them and drew her back into his arms. "This is turning out to be one terrific night."

She gazed up at him. "Daniel, be serious."

"I'm absolutely serious."

"You can't be. I was covered in flour when you arrived. I mashed your bouquet, spilled wine on your boots, put spangles in your stew and then laminated it to the bottom of the pan."

"All because you, a woman of many talents, a woman with a fair measure of fame and a considerable measure of beauty, tried to impress an average guy like me. You want to know how that makes me feel, Rose? That makes me feel pretty special."

The frown slowly disappeared from her face. "Yeah?"

"Yeah."

Gradually the spark returned to her eyes and the corners of her mouth tipped up into an endearing smile. "It's all pretty funny, when you think of it."

"You won't hear that from me."

She chuckled. "It's okay. I'm beginning to see the humor in it." She gave him an impish look. "Seems like dinner's ruined."

"Yep."

"And that *is* what I invited you up here for."

He guided her hips until they brushed against his. "Is it?"

Her eyes grew sultry again. "Maybe not entirely."

"Then let me be brutally honest. I don't give a damn about eating dinner. It wasn't your home-cooked dinner I was looking forward to when I walked in your front door."

She wound her arms around his neck and leaned into him. "Is that right?"

"That's right." His voice had a raw edge, brought on by the press of her body against his. Nobody could lean quite so sensuously as Rose, he decided.

"Well, I certainly want to be a good hostess." Her seductive glance fired his blood.

Maybe she'd practiced that look a million times for the camera, but that didn't mute its effect on him. With a groan he took possession of her saucy mouth.

She kissed him back, even as she began maneuvering them out of the kitchen. Kissing and caressing each other as they went, they made their way through the living room. She kicked off her shoes; he stripped off his belt. By the time they reached her bedroom door, he had both hands on the hem of her shirt, ready to pull it over her head.

The intercom buzzed.

"Ignore it," she said breathlessly as she raised her arms over her head.

"Thank God for a secure building." He pulled off her shirt and tossed it aside as the buzzer sounded again.

Then the phone rang.

"The machine will get it," she said, pulling him into the bedroom.

"Thank God for machines. Ah, Rose," he murmured. "You're like a piece of fine sculpture."

"Sculpture for you to mold," she said, gliding into his

arms as the answering machine beeped and prepared to accept a message.

"Miss Kingsford, I think you'd better get down here," said a male voice.

Daniel paused and looked at Rose, who had gone completely still.

"Your mother is wrestling in the lobby with a woman called Maureen," Jimmy said distinctly.

"OH, MY GOD." Rose looked around frantically for her shirt. She scooped it off the floor and pulled it over her head as she started for the apartment door.

"Rose?" Daniel seemed a little dazed.

"Put your belt on and come with me," she said, tucking her shirt into her jeans. "And button your shirt."

"You don't have any shoes on."

"Oh." She glanced down at her feet, then ran to find her shoes. After shoving her feet into them, she grabbed her keys from the table by the door and took hold of the doorknob. "Coming?" she said, looking back at Daniel.

He finished buckling his belt and started forward. "Why do I have the feeling you know what this is all about?"

"I'll tell you in the elevator. There's no time to waste. My mother works out in a gym, and she could do your mother serious damage."

"*My mother?*" He hurried after her. "What makes you think the Maureen wrestling with your mother downstairs is my Maureen?"

She slammed her hand against the elevator button. "Move, you geriatric machine!" Then she turned to him. "I was hoping none of this would have anything to do with us, but it seems your mother and mine knew each other back in Ireland."

He stared at her for a long moment. "You're not going

to tell me that your mother is Bridget Mary Hogan. I refuse to believe that.''

''Maybe the battling colleens in the lobby will convince you. Where is that blasted elevator? We should have taken the stairs. We—''

''Bridget Mary Hogan, the two-faced piece of baggage who cheated Maureen Fiona Keegan out of the Rose of Tralee crown?''

Rose glared at him. ''Watch your language or I'll be forced to mention that Maureen Fiona Keegan was the gossip-mongering, sheep-faced ne'er-do-well who cheated Bridget Mary Hogan out of the Rose of Tralee crown.'' The elevator arrived and she stepped inside, but when she turned around Daniel was still rooted to the spot.

''No. This isn't happening,'' he said in a disbelieving tone. ''Any minute I'm going to wake up.''

''You'd better wake up now and get in this blasted elevator,'' she said. ''I'll need your muscles downstairs.''

He followed her into the elevator. ''But Bridget Hogan is dead! My mother said she threw herself off the Cliffs of Moher in agony over what she'd done.''

''Yeah, well, your mother was supposed to have jumped in front of a speeding train, according to my mother.''

''Good God.'' He gazed at her as if he still couldn't comprehend the truth.

''Please button your shirt, Daniel. My mother likes to kid herself that I'm still a virgin.''

He complied, but his movements were the jerky motions of a robot. ''What else don't I know?''

That I want you to father my child, Rose thought. Now wasn't a very propitious moment to bring that up, however. ''My mother was hiding behind the planter in the tearoom when you and I first met. She was the one who insisted I go to the rendezvous with your mother. She wanted to discover how Maureen turned out.''

Daniel groaned. ''Did my mother know whose daughter you were?''

''No.'' Rose took a deep breath as the elevator clunked to a stop. ''But I suspect she does now.''

The elevator doors slid back like the curtains on a stage play. A violent stage play, Rose amended to herself. Maureen and Bridget rolled on the floor, screeching unintelligible things to each other. The match seemed to be more equal than Rose had expected. Her mother had agility, but Maureen had heft on her side, although she was hampered by the dress she wore, while Bridget's pantsuit allowed more freedom of movement.

Jimmy circled them like a referee. Every once in a while he'd dart in and make a tentative effort to stop the fighting, but he was obviously intimidated by the thought of accidentally grabbing some part of middle-aged female anatomy he was too well brought up to touch. One wing chair had been upset and the artificial-flower display was smashed into a million pieces on the floor.

Rose heard Daniel's horrified gasp, but he apparently had command of himself almost immediately.

''I'll get them apart,'' he said. ''Then we'll each take our own. Get the kid to help you if you can't hold your mother yourself.''

''Got it.'' Rose watched in admiration as Daniel waded into the fray. She winced as Bridget's foot connected with his stomach. If the kick had been a little lower, he might have been rendered out of action.

''Okay, ladies,'' he said in a voice that rang with authority. ''Let's break it up now, shall we?''

''It's my Daniel!'' screeched Maureen. ''Daniel, get this madwoman off me!''

"I think technically you're on top of her." He pulled both women to their feet and wedged his body between them. "Rose? Jimmy? Can I get a hand, here?"

Rose bolted forward and clutched her mother's arm. "Come over here, Mom." She tugged, but Bridget planted both feet. She was stronger than Rose had expected.

"Maureen Fiona, you're no better than a pimp!" she shouted across Daniel.

"Hah!" Maureen shouted back. "I'd rather see my Daniel marry a duck in Central Park than any daughter of yours, Bridget Mary!"

"Okay, ladies, let's each go to our respective corners," Daniel said, putting both arms around his mother and maneuvering her a few feet away.

Rose felt her mother wriggling out of her grasp. "Jimmy, could you help me?"

Jimmy approached nervously. "Excuse me, Mrs. Kingsford," he said apologetically as he put a hammerlock on her neck.

"Very good, Jimmy," Rose said.

"He's choking the life out of me!" Bridget yelped.

"What a lovely idea," Rose muttered in her mother's ear. "What in hell are you doing here?"

"Don't you dare accuse me of wrongdoing, young lady! There's razor burn on your cheek!"

Rose struggled not to feel like a teenager caught coming home late from a torrid date with her steady. She lowered her voice. "I'm thirty years old, for heaven's sake!"

"Old enough to know better than to fool around with the likes of Maureen Keegan's son!"

"I heard that!" shouted Maureen from across the room. "Nobody insults my Daniel. I'll—"

"Not now, Mom," Daniel said. "Rose, I think we need a couple of cabs."

"I'll call," Rose offered. She marveled at his even tone of voice. She glanced across the room where he held his disheveled mother in a bear hug. When he was alone with his mother he'd probably chew her up one side and down the other, as Rose planned to do with her own mother. At the moment, however, he was reacting like a perfectly trained cop. Rose admired his self-possession.

Rose glanced at Jimmy. "Got her?"

"I've got her," Jimmy said, looking very determined. "Miss Kingsford, I don't know what the owners are going to say about this mess."

"Don't worry, Jimmy. I'll testify that it wasn't your fault that things got out of hand." She walked to the phone and dialed the number for the cab company she used. "My mother will pay for the damage."

"Me?" Bridget shrieked. "What about herself over there? None of this would have happened if she hadn't spread those terrible lies about me to the contest judges!"

Rose covered the ear that wasn't against the phone and ordered two cabs.

"You *deliberately* burned my face, you did!" Maureen tried to struggle out of Daniel's grip. "Daniel, are you going to let her speak to your mother like that?"

"Actually, I'm tempted to let you go and then call for the SWAT team," Daniel said.

Rose caught the barely leashed anger in his words. "Cabs are on the way," she said.

"Good. I think we'll wait outside."

"But 'tis raining cats and dogs out there," his mother protested.

"Sounds perfect. I'd also contemplated turning a fire hose on both of you."

"Daniel, your jacket," Rose said, realizing it was still up in her apartment.

"I'll get it later." With one brief glance at Rose, Daniel escorted his mother out the revolving door.

Rose took some comfort from his last remark, but not much. Retrieving his jacket at some future date wasn't exactly the same as continuing a relationship. She couldn't imagine he'd want that now. After all, the idea had been for them to enjoy an uncomplicated, sexy time together. This was turning out to be unbelievably complicated.

"She's gone. You can turn me loose, Jimmy," Bridget said.

"Don't you do it, Jimmy." Rose faced the source of all her troubles with renewed anger. "What were you doing here, spying on me?"

Even with a rip in the sleeve of her London Fog raincoat, a big black smudge on the knee of her designer slacks, and wildly tangled hair—and despite the fact that Jimmy held her in an uncompromising hammerlock— Bridget managed to look haughty. "I was merely checking to see if you were home. I'd just managed to get some tickets to a concert at the Kennedy Center, the tribute to that jazz musician you like, and I wanted to tell you right away. I was in the neighborhood, so naturally—"

"Bull."

"Rose, your language is shocking."

"I'm using restraint, Mom. Believe me, I could come up with several expressions that are a lot more crude, and they all apply."

"Looks like the cabs are outside, Miss Kingsford," Jimmy said, his voice charged with relief.

"Tell me when one has left with Daniel and his mother in it."

"He's shoving her—uh, I mean *helping* her into one now. There it goes."

"Okay. Mom, if Jimmy lets you go, do you promise to walk with me out to the cab?"

"There's no need to take that tone with me, Rose Erin Kingsford. Your grandmother would turn over in her—"

"No doubt Granny's spinning like a top in her grave," Rose said. "And I'm not taking any of the credit for it, either. You're the one who was brawling in the lobby of the apartment building. Now do you promise to get in the cab with me?"

"I promise."

Rose nodded to Jimmy and he relaxed his hammerlock and stepped back.

Bridget brushed at her clothes and patted her tangled hair. It looked as if Maureen had wound her fingers through it several times. "You don't need to ride in the cab, Rose," Bridget said as she started toward the door. "I'll go straight home."

"I think I'll just tag along, anyway." Rose fell into step beside her. "We have a few things to straighten out."

"You don't have a coat."

"As hot under the collar as I am at the moment, I don't need one, Mom. Let's just go."

"Take mine." Bridget started to pull off her London Fog.

"No, thanks." Rose helped her mother back on with the coat as she guided her toward the door. "I'm furious with you, but I wouldn't forgive myself if you caught a chill."

"What you're going to give me is a heart attack."

"Nonsense." The cold, wet air felt great as they walked outside and Rose took a deep breath. "Your heart is fine. Anybody who can wrestle Maureen Keegan to the ground is in pretty good shape, if you ask me."

Her mother stooped to climb into the back seat of the

cab. Then she glanced over her shoulder. "I would have had her begging for mercy in another five minutes."

Rose rolled her eyes. "I've decided you must be related to Hulk Hogan. I'm signing you up for the World Wrestling Federation Championships tomorrow." As she climbed in the cab she heard the strangest snorting sounds coming from her mother. Finally she figured out what it was. Her mother was trying to control an uncontrollable belly laugh. Rose leaned her head against the cracked upholstery and sighed. "Go ahead, Mom. Let it out."

Bridget laughed until the tears streamed down her face. "You should have seen her expression when I told her who I was," she gasped. "You'd have thought somebody had whacked her between the eyes with a sledgehammer. Jesus, Mary and Joseph, but it was a great moment. I'd have given anything for a camera."

"Actually, I imagine we have footage of the whole episode," Rose said, smiling in spite of herself. "There's that little closed-circuit camera mounted above Jimmy's desk."

Still laughing, Bridget clutched Rose's arm. "You simply *must* get me that tape. It will carry me happily into my old age. I just wish I'd had another five minutes to pin her to the floor."

Rose turned her head to look at her mother. "You're really sorry we interrupted you?"

"I've been waiting to get into a donnybrook with that woman my whole life. When we were girls we thought we were much too dignified for physical violence."

"Thank God you don't have your dignity to protect anymore."

"Rose, are you being sarcastic?"

"Who, me?"

"Well, at least we interrupted you two," Bridget said,

"which was probably more important than finishing the fight good and proper. I don't suppose you'll be getting involved with Maureen Keegan O'Malley's son. She'll threaten him with everything, including excommunication, if he continues to see you."

Rose sighed. "I doubt if she'll need to threaten him at all, Mom. After this display tonight, he'll probably want to stay as far away from me as possible."

Bridget patted her hand. "That's for the best, Rose. Especially if you had in mind what I think you did." She shivered. "Talk about a fate worse than death. If I thought Maureen Keegan and I would be grandmothers to the same child, I'd have to throw myself off the Empire State Building."

"Have you forgotten you have a fear of heights?"

Bridget gave her a long look. "I'd overcome it."

6

IT WAS A LONG cab ride to Brooklyn, but Daniel figured he'd let his mother pay for every mile. Still, furious as he was, he hoped she hadn't done herself any physical damage wrestling with Rose's mother. Wrestling in a public lobby. Sweet Jesus. And he'd thought she couldn't embarrass him any more than she had in the tearoom. At this rate he'd have to reduce his hours on the force just so he could keep an eye on her.

"Are you all right?" he asked after several moments of tense silence.

"She scared the life out of me, she did!" His mother fiddled with a button on her wool coat. "Tore the armhole seam of my coat, too."

"I don't give a damn about the coat. I just want to know if you pulled a muscle or broke anything."

His mother made a sound of disgust. "'Twould be a fine day when Bridget Hogan could overtake me in a fight. Did you see that I had the best of her, Daniel? She would have been begging for mercy in another two minutes."

From the vehemence and spirit of his mother's reply, Daniel decided only her dignity was damaged. And he obviously cared about that more than she did. "Bridget has a pretty good kick for somebody who's been dead for thirty-seven years," he said.

"'Tis just like you to bring that little matter up to me

at a time like this. 'Twas nothing but an innocent pretense.''

''Innocent? Lying to Dad and me in great detail about how she flung herself off the cliffs because she couldn't live with the way she'd treated you in that beauty contest? What's so innocent about that?''

''Well, she should have done it.''

Daniel turned sideways on the seat so he could confront her more directly. ''Don't tell me you still hold a grudge.''

His mother glared at him defiantly. In the dim light of the cab he could almost believe she'd transformed herself into a rebellious teenager. ''She never said she was sorry, did she, now?''

Daniel closed his eyes. ''Unbelievable.''

''And it's not enough that she ruined the years when I was a tender bud ready to blossom forth in all my glory. Now she's ruined my golden years, too!''

''And how did she do that?'' Daniel was having trouble following the tortured reasoning of this woman he thought he knew.

His mother shook her head. ''At times I wonder if the sisters mixed up your test scores with some other lad's. You're not quick on the uptake sometimes, Daniel.''

''Then I guess you'll just have to lay it out for me.''

''Well, 'tis perfectly plain. Just how are you and Rose supposed to get married, now that Rose has turned out to be the daughter of that back-stabbing conniver? Answer me that!''

He stared at her. Then finally he began to laugh. He laughed so hard he almost choked.

His mother looked alarmed. ''Are you having a fit, Daniel?''

''No.'' He took a long, steadying breath. ''Just enjoying the irony of the situation. Maybe this will put an end to this wife-hunting you've been so hell-bent on. I couldn't have planned this better if I'd tried.''

"'Tis fine for you to laugh, but you're not thinking of your poor mother at all. No grandchildren to gather around me in my declining years, no young woman I can teach the ways of an Irish housewife—the knitting, the cooking, the gardening.''

"Since when did you have a garden?''

"Never mind. I know how to garden. You don't forget those things, once you learn them. But it doesn't matter, you see, because there'll be no garden, no family pictures, no sweet little birthday parties, no Christmas carols around the tree, no—''

"I think you're getting a little carried away, Mom.'' He paused. "Not that it's anything new with you these days.''

"You think you're so smart. Just wait until you're fifty-six, with no family to comfort you!''

Daniel decided to shift the subject a little. "So I take it you don't want me to see Rose Kingsford after all?''

"Well, of course I don't!'' She clasped a hand to her chest and looked at him in horror. "Bridget Hogan weaseling her way into *our* family, pinching the dear little cheek of *my* grandchild? I can just see the shameless hussy, spoiling the dear thing with too many toys, too many sweets. She'd probably make up some sickening pet name for the babe, like Nana's wee elf, and I'd have to listen to her calling my little darling that awful name. She'd—''

"I take it that's a no?''

"I'd sooner be struck down by a bolt of lightning than have you marry Rose Kingsford!''

"Well, you can put your mind at rest, because I'm not going to marry Rose.'' He leaned back against the seat and folded his arms over his chest.

"Thank heavens you've come to your senses.''

"We'll just fool around."

His mother gasped and clutched her chest again. "Oh, no, you wouldn't be doin' *that* now, would you?"

Daniel faced her again, his expression grim. "If it hadn't been for your interference, I wouldn't have met Rose. But I have met her, and if I decide to continue seeing her, I most definitely will. In fact, if I decided to marry her, I'd do that, too. But it's your good luck that I'm not looking for a wife, and Rose, coincidentally, is not looking for a husband."

"Oh, Daniel, please don't say that you two will—"

"Don't worry. I won't say it. That's not the sort of topic I want to discuss with you. I want this to be the very last time we talk about who I date and who I do or don't marry. This has gone on long enough."

"I just can't bear to think of it."

"Then don't think of it." Daniel leaned back and closed his eyes. "Butt out of my business, Mom."

ROSE WAS EXTREMELY grateful to be working with her buddy Chuck the following day. The modeling assignment involved shots of a honeymooning couple, alias Rose and Chuck, enjoying the wonders of a Gold Card. Tall, blond and muscled in all the right places, Chuck looked like every woman's dream of the perfect guy to have on a honeymoon. And he'd just moved in with Pete, his lover of several months.

Rose cherished that she wouldn't be pawed during the shooting, and that she'd have an intelligent companion during breaks. Besides, she needed advice, and Chuck was well versed in the ways of the heart. It took all of the first break just to fill him in on the bizarre situation with her mother and Daniel's mother, so they didn't get down to the advice session until lunch.

Over a catered meal of deli sandwiches and mineral water consumed in a corner of the photography studio's deserted conference room, Rose asked Chuck what she should do next.

"Meaning you want to see him again?" Chuck asked. "In spite of the fact it will throw these two middle-aged ladies into fits, and they in turn could make your life miserable beyond words?"

"Yes."

"And that would be because...?"

"Well, I still have his jacket."

"You could courier that to him. Next reason."

"He's very sweet, and sexy, and he has more than two brain cells to rub together."

"That's a rare combination. Are you sure he's straight?"

"Chuck, believe it or not, there are a few heterosexual men out there who aren't jerks."

Chuck smiled. "Yeah, and a few gay guys who are. I'm happy for you, Rose."

"You can't be happy for me yet. He may have sworn off Rose Kingsford for life after last night. He wanted an uncomplicated relationship, and this is turning out to be anything but."

"And what do you want, Rose?"

"The same thing." She couldn't admit, not even to Chuck, that she harbored a dream of finding someone to father her child. Her mother had been the only one she'd told, and that had brought on a storm of judgment.

Chuck swallowed a bite of sandwich. "There's no such thing as an uncomplicated relationship unless you're talking about a dog."

"Okay, I'll admit that." Rose took a drink from the bottle of mineral water. "But neither of us wants a commitment. No rings, no march down the aisle. We got that settled right away.''

"So it's just about sex, then?"

"You are so hard on me! Of course not! It's about companionship, and mutual interests, and—"

"Such as?"

"Well, we—" She gave him a sheepish look. "So far it's about sex.''

Chuck nodded. "Just so you're not confused about that.''

"Actually, let me amend my statement a little bit. It's about mutual respect, too. We've already weathered a few awkward situations, and he's good under fire.''

"I sure as hell hope so. I like that in a member of the NYPD.''

"I know, but more than that. He saw me at my worst and didn't get upset at all. I sense that he's a kind person.''

"That's good. So are you.''

"I don't think he'd blame me for what happened between our mothers, but I don't know if he wants the hassle of risking it again.''

Chuck wadded up his deli sack and tossed a perfect basket into the nearby trash can. "Want Uncle Chuck to suggest something?"

"Please.''

"Invite him up to your little place in the country for a few days. And don't tell the mothers.''

Rose swirled the remaining mineral water and stared at the miniature whirlpool she'd created. "I don't know. He made a point of the difference in our income, and how he didn't want to be included in plans that were out of his financial league.''

"Well, I don't see that a visit to your little house would fall into that category, but if you think he'll balk, tell him a friend offered the place. His stance will probably soften some if you two have a great time together. Pete gave me the same garbage at first, and I thought we'd have to live in a rat-infested walk-up because that was all he could afford in the city. We've finally worked it out.''

"I guess that attitude's better than linking up with a gold digger, huh?''

"You know it. We'd better get back, kiddo.''

"Yeah. Thanks, Chuck.''

He stood. "Ready for the honeymoon?''

She blinked. "I said neither of us is interested in marriage.''

Chuck gazed at her, a glint in his blue eyes. "I meant yours and mine, courtesy of a Gold Card. But it's rather interesting that you misunderstood.''

"Don't you dare make something Freudian out of it. I do not have some subliminal desire to settle down with a man and be his devoted helpmate.''

"If you say so.''

On Wednesday, Daniel took an early shift, switching with a buddy. During the day, whenever there was a lag in the action, Daniel thought of Rose. When he got home that afternoon he reached for the phone a hundred times. Each time he pulled his hand back before committing to the call. No matter what he'd said to his mother, he wasn't sure he wanted to pursue a relationship with such a problematic woman. Their two mothers were only part of his reluctance.

The sizzle of chemistry between them had blocked out his surroundings for the most part the previous night, but enough had registered to make him decide that this woman had money. A *lot* of money, compared to him. He realized now that he'd dated only women who were approximately his economic equals. He'd never thought it would bother him to go out with someone financially better off than he was, but…it did. He wasn't proud to find out he was so hidebound, but there it was. He sensed a bedrock of prejudice that might take a nuclear blast to dislodge.

He'd finally decided to head out for a movie, when the phone rang. He stepped back into the apartment and answered it to discover Rose on the other end. She might have thought she'd get the answering machine, he realized when she seemed startled to hear his voice. She was probably calling about his jacket.

"I can hang up and let the machine get the message if you'd rather make this less personal," he said.

"Don't tempt me," she said. "You wouldn't believe how difficult it was for me to pick up the phone in the first place."

"I might."

"Listen, you can just send the jacket—"

"Oh, the jacket. I forgot. Do you need it?"

He was glad to know that wasn't why she'd called. "No rush."

"Because I can courier it over."

"It's not important, Rose. So if you didn't call about the jacket, why did you call?"

She took a deep breath. "Daniel, we've run into a bad patch right at the start."

"Yep."

"I probably should have told you all about our mothers from the beginning."

"Probably."

"Come on, Daniel, work with me, here. Don't leave me out on this limb all by myself."

He blew out a breath. "Okay. I've thought about calling you about a million times since last night."

"But you didn't."

"I had a lot to think about."

"I realize that. Discovering that I was the daughter of your mother's dearest enemy must have come as a shock."

He couldn't help laughing. "Dearest enemy is right. She's positively devoted to this thirty-seven-year-old grudge."

"So's my mother. And she's determined I won't have anything more to do with you."

He hesitated. "That's not why you're calling, is it? To show her who's boss?"

"No. I hope I've gotten past that kind of adolescent behavior."

"Which is more than they have."

"True," Rose said. "They're acting like a couple of naughty children, which is why I don't want to be ruled by their lunacy. I'd...I'd like to see you again," she finished in a rush.

He knew she needed an answer, but he wasn't sure which one he wanted to give her.

"Your silence is eloquent," she said. "I don't blame you for wanting to end the relationship. Goodbye, Daniel."

"Wait!"

"Yes?"

His heart pounded, as if he'd had to physically chase her down. "I'd like to see you again, too."

"You would?"

Her question lacked the bubbling confidence he'd become so fond of, and it was his fault. "Yes, I would. Forgive me for making you doubt it, or yourself. It's my problem, not yours."

"Your mother?"

"No, not my mother. It's—" He swallowed and forced himself to admit it. "It's your success. But it just occurred to me that only a fool would turn his back on someone like you because of stupid macho pride.''

''You didn't seem too concerned about my success last night,'' she said gently.

''Exactly. I don't think our income levels will have much to do with anything when we make love.''

She greeted that statement with a quick intake of breath. ''And will we make love, Daniel?''

''If I haven't completely turned you off with my idiot attitudes, we will.''

''You, um, haven't turned me off.'' She sounded a little breathless.

Just like that, he was becoming aroused. ''Are you free tonight?''

''No. I promised my mother we'd go to a ballet. I could—''

''Don't chance it. I've told my mother to stay out of my business, but I'm not sure I trust her to do it.''

''I've given my mother the same orders, but she's acting like a crazy woman over this. Which is why I thought perhaps, if we could go away somewhere....''

Daniel felt his defenses go up immediately. Was she planning on jetting them both to a lovers' hideaway? Despite his resolve not to let her money bother him, he couldn't be treated like some gigolo and retain his sense of himself. ''Where?'' he asked with deceptive calmness.

''A...person I know has a little cottage upstate. We're welcome to use it. If you'll tell me when you're off duty, I'll try to arrange my schedule around that. We can drive there in a couple of hours.''

''It just so happens I have Friday through Sunday off, one of those rare weekends.'' He suspected there was more to this cottage business than she was telling him, but the way she'd phrased everything, he could deal with it. And there was no denying he was eager to spend time alone with her.

"That's perfect! I don't have any assignments this weekend, either. I have a tentative thing on Friday, but I can probably reschedule it for Monday."

He realized they were talking about leaving in less than two days. His blood began to heat at the prospect of all that delicious time alone with Rose. If, in fact, they could be alone. "Does your mother know where this cottage is?"

"I know what you're thinking, but we don't have to worry about her bursting in on us. She's been there, but I doubt she could find it by herself. Besides, she doesn't drive. We'd be safe."

"She could hire a car."

"I suppose, but she'd never be able to direct them to the place, which would embarrass her, so I can't believe she'd try it. It's very rural and there's no address. The owner picks up her mail at the post office in town. Not many people in town know she has the place."

He was pretty sure the owner was Rose Kingsford, but he decided not to press her. She was trying to find a way for them to be alone together, and her solution was better than any he could come up with. His apartment wouldn't work because his mother had a key. He should probably change that, although he didn't look forward to her tearful reaction, and then she wouldn't have a haven when she came into the city to go shopping.

"Well?" Rose asked.

He'd kept her waiting—again. "Sorry. I was thinking."

"Look, if you have doubts, I'll just hang up and that will be the end of it. I said I wouldn't blame you, and I won't."

"I'd like to go up to the cottage with you, Rose. I'd like that very much."

She gave a relieved little sigh. "Good."

"And I'll drive."

"You have a car? I mean, not that you couldn't afford one," she amended quickly. "It's just that lots of people in the city—"

"I have a car." He didn't even want to know what kind she had. "And why don't I bring some food along, too?"

"Food?"

He smiled to himself. "Just in case we find the time to eat."

"Oh!"

He could almost see her cheeks turning the color of her name, and his smile broadened. "Then again, maybe we could just pop a few vitamin pills and save time. I'm not picky."

"Well, of course we'll eat," she said, sounding out of breath. "But there's stuff up there, I'm sure."

The comment about the food clinched it for him. It was her house, no doubt about it. She'd called it a cottage but it could be a country mansion for all he knew. He kept up the pretense because it allowed him to contribute more to the weekend. "You wouldn't want to eat your friend's food supply, would you?"

"I guess that wouldn't be a good idea. Sure, bring whatever you like. That'll be fine."

He couldn't resist. "And whatever I know how to cook?"

"Hey."

He chuckled. "Sorry. The devil made me say it. I'll make sure whatever I bring is a no-brainer." He paused. "I see no reason to spend lots of time in the kitchen."

Another quick intake of breath told him she'd begun to envision where they would spend most of their time. He was envisioning it, too, and his whole body was beginning to hum in anticipation of holding her again. "I'll pick you up about nine, so we'll miss the rush-hour traffic."

"Sounds great. By the way, I'll probably make up some story to tell my mother about where I'll be this weekend, but I travel a lot, so it shouldn't be too difficult. How about you?"

"I've told my mother to stay out of my business."

She hesitated. "I see."

"You don't sound convinced that she will."

"I can only judge by my mother, who doesn't exactly take orders well. But maybe your mother is different. Maybe that authoritarian cop voice had an impact."

He laughed. "What authoritarian cop voice?"

"The one you used when you waded into the wrestling match. If somebody spoke to me in that tone of voice, I'd probably pay attention."

"Remind me to try it sometime."

"I said probably. I'm also my mother's daughter."

"Which is why we're sneaking around like this. Okay, in the interests of securing an uninterrupted weekend I'll tell my mother I'm attending an intensive three-day course on riot control. We have St. Patrick's Day coming up, so that's a logical story."

"This feels so illicit."

"I hope to hell that's not what's motivating you, because if it is, then maybe we shouldn't—"

"Hey, Daniel, remember how we reacted to each other last night?"

"Yeah." He took a shaky breath. "I do."

"That's what's motivating me. See you Friday morning. I'll bring your jacket."

"As if I'll be needing it."

7

ON AN IMPULSE, Rose brought along some tapes of Irish folk songs for the drive to her cottage. She'd bought copies for herself and her mother during her recent trip to Ireland, and they'd become her favorite music. To her surprise, Daniel enjoyed them as much as she did, and even knew the words to a few of the more familiar ones.

"You have a great voice!" she announced after the first song they did together.

"But it's a baritone. I was supposed to be an Irish tenor. My grandfather was a tenor and my uncle was a tenor. When my voice changed and it became obvious I wouldn't be a tenor, my mother went into mourning."

Rose laughed. "Tradition is a blessing and a curse, isn't it?"

"Especially for the Irish."

"Oh, listen. It's 'The Titanic.' I used to sing that at camp when I was a kid."

Daniel grinned at her. "Didn't everybody?"

They belted out the song about the great ship going down, and followed it with a schmaltzy rendition of "Danny Boy," while a light snow fell all around them. Traffic was about as heavy as usual on 87 for a Friday, but Daniel drove his Toyota Supra with practiced ease. Rose couldn't remember the last time she'd felt so safe and secure.

They sang "When Irish Eyes Are Smiling," and laughed when they stumbled over the words.

"My mother would kill me for not knowing that one better," Daniel said when the song ended. "It's one of her favorites."

"One of my mother's, too."

"That figures." Daniel pulled around a slow-moving truck. "It's too bad they can't give up this stupid grudge and be friends. They have so many things in common."

"That's true." Rose contemplated what would happen if her mother and Maureen O'Malley became friends. Considering that Daniel was Rose's prime candidate for fathering a child, a chummy relationship between Maureen and Bridget wouldn't be such a great idea. In some ways the feud contributed to the overall plan. Yet she pictured vividly how a friendship with Maureen could enrich Bridget's life. An unselfish daughter would foster that friendship, not discourage it for her own reasons. Life became more complicated every minute, thought Rose as she listened to the opening chords of "My Wild Irish Rose" on the tape player.

She'd opened her mouth to sing along—she certainly knew that one after having her mother sing it to her all the time—but instinct told her to remain silent.

Daniel glanced at her with a half smile and launched into the song in his rich baritone.

No man had ever sung to her before, let alone a song that spoke of such tender love. She tried to tell herself that the words meant nothing, that Daniel was simply singing lyrics he knew well because of his Irish upbringing. Her heart was unconvinced by logic. And when he reached over and interlaced his fingers with hers, her heart believed every word.

By the time he'd finished the song, Rose had lapsed into a dreamy state that hadn't captured her in a very long time. Snuggled back against the bucket seat, she gazed at Daniel with pleasure. She would have this beautiful man all to herself for the next two days.

"What was that exit again?" he asked.

Rose jerked out of her trance and looked at a highway sign right at the moment they zoomed beyond the turnoff to her little hideaway. "We, uh, just passed it. I'm sorry, Daniel. There's another exit in three miles."

He grinned. "Hey, don't apologize. When a woman misses the highway exit because she's staring adoringly at me, how can I be upset?"

She bolted to an upright position. "I was not staring adoringly!"

"Were too. Admit it—that song made you all dewy-eyed."

"So the song has some meaning for me. Just because you happened to be the one singing it doesn't mean that I—"

"You don't have to get so defensive." He winked at her. "I enjoyed the admiration."

"Is this my reward for complimenting you on your singing voice? Are you now going to become insufferably vain and think that all you have to do is warble a few notes and I'll become hypnotized and do whatever you want?"

"I call 'em like I see 'em. You looked totally captivated to me."

She rolled her eyes. "With an ego that huge, I'm surprised you had room in this car for me and the luggage."

Daniel just smiled at her, and when "Peg O' My Heart" started playing, he sang while giving her soulful looks.

"You're impossible!" But she couldn't help laughing as he continued to clown around for her benefit.

They turned off at the next exit. As Daniel flicked on the car's turn signal in preparation for driving beneath the underpass and back onto the highway, Rose spotted a hand-lettered sign nailed to a fencepost about a hundred feet to the right. The Gentle Giants—Irish Wolfhound Puppies For Sale, announced the sign, and an arrow pointed down a country road.

"Wait." Rose put a hand on Daniel's arm. "See that sign?"

He hunched down and peered out the windshield. "Puppies?"

"I think we should go look at them."

"At puppies?"

A driver behind them honked his car's horn in obvious impatience.

"It won't take long. I promise."

Daniel shrugged and flipped on the right-turn signal. "I don't care about that. I just wonder why you want to go see puppies." He headed the car down the country road.

"I've wanted an Irish wolfhound for years. And here's somebody right in my area who raises them."

"In your area, you say?"

She could tell from the penetrating look in those brown eyes of his that he'd guessed the truth. She sighed. "Okay, the cottage belongs to me. But it's not all paid for," she added quickly. She didn't tell him that the renovations were the part still being paid off. She'd paid cash for the original building and land.

"How big is it?" he asked as they followed another sign that pointed down a narrow lane bordered by a white fence.

"Small. Very small." That much was true—three tiny bedrooms, a small kitchen only big enough for a table for two, one bathroom and a cozy living-dining room combination. But the custom thatched roof and leaded-glass windows had cost her a fortune.

"I guess a small house in the country isn't quite the same as a villa in the south of France." He pulled up in front of a two-story farmhouse with a deep red hay barn to the rear of the property. "This must be where your puppy lives."

"I'm not getting one right now," she said. "I just want to make the contact and find out when they'll have another litter ready to sell."

Daniel grabbed his leather jacket and her trench coat from the back seat. "Then we're not going inside?" he asked, handing her the coat.

"Of course we're going inside. I want to see the puppies, even if I'm not getting one today."

He reached for the door handle. "I can tell you're not an experienced puppy shopper."

"What do you mean?"

He paused and gazed at her. "If you were, you'd get the information at the front door, then leave."

"That's crazy! Why wouldn't I want to see what sort of puppies they breed?"

"Because you'll leave with one."

"I certainly will not. This is a preliminary visit, for heaven's sake. Don't you credit me with any willpower?"

He leaned toward her. "Nobody has any willpower when it comes to puppies."

"Well, I do."

"We'll see." He gave her a quick kiss and climbed out of the car.

AN HOUR LATER they pulled back onto the highway, a pet carrier in the back seat and a sheepish grin on Rose's face.

Daniel didn't have the heart to rub it in. He'd damn near picked out a puppy himself, although the price tag would have stopped him from doing something that stupid. The breeder had taken them back to the hay barn where ten puppies played happily among the chickens. Although at thirty-five pounds the eight-week-old puppies were big enough to kill a hen, they showed no desire to do that. Daniel had never seen such gentle animals.

When Rose crouched down, all the puppies had headed for her, but a tan male had put his front paws on her knee and reached up to give her a kiss on the cheek. Daniel had watched with indulgence and a trace of jealousy as Rose fell in love.

The breeder had loaned them the pet carrier and given them a few cans of dog food. She'd cautioned them about letting the puppy sleep in their bed tonight.

"You won't be able to bear the pitiful crying," she'd said, "but you'll start that habit at your peril. This dog will gain a half pound a day and eventually weigh around two-fifty. He'll own that bed."

Daniel was grateful for the tip. No matter how cute the puppy, Daniel didn't want him in bed with them tonight. He had other plans.

As if on cue, the little guy began to whimper as the car picked up speed.

Rose twisted in her seat so she could peer through the wire grate of the carrier. "It's okay, St. Paddy. You're going to be fine," she crooned. "Just fine."

St. Paddy stopped whimpering at the sound of her voice, but the minute she stopped talking to him he started up again.

"Easy, my little love," she murmured. "We'll be home before you know it."

Daniel was enchanted by her tone of voice as she comforted the puppy. Enchanted and somewhat worried. He wondered how much attention he'd get this weekend, now that St. Paddy was in the picture. Yet, realizing what joy having the puppy gave Rose, he wouldn't have dreamed of protesting.

"It was fate that we missed the exit," Rose said.

"Then I guess it was my fantastic singing that provided you with this dog."

"All right. I'll confess," she began, "if you promise to be just as truthful to me."

"I'm always truthful."

"Okay, it *was* your singing that...distracted me."

"In a good way or a bad way?"

"A good way. There, there, little Paddy," she reassured the puppy as he began crying again.

"That's what I figured." Actually he hadn't been sure. He'd surprised himself, getting all sentimental with that song, but it fit Rose so perfectly that he'd gotten a little carried away. It was nice to know he'd carried her away, too.

"Now it's my turn," she said. "How many women named Rose have you worked that little number on?"

"None."

She murmured a few soothing words to the puppy before turning back to him. "None? An Irish stud like you?"

He grinned. "If you think you're going to goad me into admitting something, you're wrong. I've never met anybody else named Rose except Rose Conners, a sweet but very old lady who was the church organist when I was a kid in the choir."

"Ha. Rose Conners was probably twenty-five and you seduced her in the choir loft."

He took the exit they'd missed before. "Where are you getting this idea that I'm some sort of Don Juan?"

"You didn't kiss me after our first date. You kissed me *before* our first date. I suppose you'll tell me that doesn't happen all the time, either."

"Not often." He decided not to tell her he'd never kissed a woman so soon after meeting her. But the night he came upon Rose standing outside the restaurant she'd looked like some heavenly being temporarily touching down to dazzle earthbound men. The streetlight had transformed the rain falling all around her into a shower of diamonds, and he'd had to kiss her to convince himself that she was real.

"It happens often enough, I'll bet. That was a very experienced kind of kiss," she said. "Okay, turn right at the stop sign and slow down as we go through the town. They put speeders in the stocks around here."

"What do you mean by *experienced?*"

She smiled. "Worried about your technique, are you?"

"No, I—oh, hell." Red and blue lights flashed in the rearview mirror.

"I warned you."

So she had, and he'd been thinking about kissing her and hadn't paid attention. "This is damned embarrassing." He pulled off to the side of the road and extracted his wallet from his hip pocket.

"I think it's kind of funny, a cop running afoul of the law."

"This isn't running afoul of the law. I was just keeping up with traffic."

"What traffic? The road was practically deserted."

"Which made it difficult to judge my speed."

"Tell it to the judge," Rose said, grinning.

Daniel scowled at her before rolling down the window and glancing up at the patrolman approaching the driver's side of the car.

The patrolman asked for Daniel's license and registration, which Daniel handed out the window to him. After glancing at it, the officer started to laugh. "Daniel Patrick O'Malley."

Daniel gritted his teeth and gave the officer his most

intimidating cop stare. Then his eyes widened as he recognized Tim Bettencourt from his graduating class at the police academy. "Tim?"

The patrolman took off his dark glasses and held out his hand. "Hey, bro. It's been a few years. How're you doin'?"

"A lot better than I was two minutes ago. I'd forgotten you took a job up here after you left the NYPD." Daniel shook his former classmate's hand and introduced him to Rose.

"We've met," Rose said.

"Nice to see you again, Rose."

Daniel opened the car door. "Let's discuss this little matter out there," he said, grabbing his jacket. "I'll only be a minute," he said in an undertone to Rose as he rolled up the car window. "Old Tim's not gonna give me a ticket, but he might not want to say so in front of you."

WHEN DANIEL CLOSED the car door, St. Paddy began to whine and paw at the wire door to his carrier.

"Soon you'll be out of there, little guy," Rose said. "Right after Daniel gets his ticket fixed we'll be heading down the road toward home. Or what will be home by the time you're too big for my apartment." She'd made some rapid calculations after she'd realized she couldn't leave the hay barn without this particular puppy with the big brown eyes. Her lease was up in three months, so by the time St. Paddy became too huge for apartment living, she'd be moved permanently to the country. In the meantime, she'd ask her mother to dog-sit during the day once in a while.

St. Paddy kept pawing at the wire and whining.

Rose leaned down to peer through the window and couldn't see much sign of the party breaking up outside.

St. Paddy sounded as if he'd lost his best friend, which, in fact, he had. All his friends were gone, replaced by two strangers.

"Okay, I'll let you out, but you'd better be good," she instructed as she slowly unlatched the door.

St. Paddy came wriggling out with surprising speed. She made a grab for him but he squirmed out of her arms and leaped neatly onto Daniel's seat. Then he squatted and a growing stain appeared on the seat cover.

"St. Paddy, no!" Rose pulled him back into her lap just as Daniel opened the car door and tossed his jacket in the back.

"Daniel! Don't—"

He sat. And lifted up again immediately. "What the...?"

She held tight to the struggling puppy. "I'm afraid that St. Paddy..."

Holding on to the steering wheel so he could elevate his behind away from the wet seat, Daniel gazed over at her. "Lady, your dog leaks."

"I'm really sorry." She bit her lip against the awful urge to laugh. "You were taking so long, and he wanted so much to get out of the carrier."

"I can see why. He had business to take care of."

"Do you have a towel or anything in the trunk?"

"I think so. You'd better get him back in the carrier before I open this door, though."

"You're right." Rose leaned over the back of the seat and tried to maneuver the puppy inside the carrier. It was like putting toothpaste back in the tube. "Sorry. He doesn't want to go in."

"Take your time. I'll just hang out here."

"Daniel, I don't know if I can do this. He's stronger than I thought."

"Try grabbing him by the scruff of the neck. Like his mother would do if she wanted to move him. Then maybe you can back him in."

"Easier said than done." But she managed it. "Coast is clear," she said, snapping the door shut.

Daniel got out of the car with some difficulty, but he returned quickly with a blanket which he folded several times before placing it on the seat.

"You don't have anything more ratty than that?" Rose asked.

"Nope." He eased onto the seat, closed the door and fastened his seat belt.

"That looks too good for the purpose."

"It is." He started the engine. "There are all kinds of sentimental memories attached to it."

"Oh, dear. I'll bet your mother gave it to you."

He grinned at her. "Nope. Picked this baby out myself when I was about seventeen. It was carefully selected for durability, washability, and a soft, fluffy nap."

"You went through all that trouble for a blanket for your bed?"

"No, a blanket for my car. And it's been transferred to each car I've owned. It's my make-out blanket."

She groaned. "I should have guessed. And here you were pretending that you're not hell on wheels with women."

"I'm not hell on wheels, Rose." He winked at her. "But I've been told I'm heaven on a blanket."

8

DANIEL'S COMMENT about being heaven on a blanket set off a predictable reaction in Rose. She couldn't remember ever having such an intense response to a man as she had to Daniel. She expected to enjoy their lovemaking very much. What she hadn't expected, or even counted on, was that he'd be great company during the times when they weren't involved in the physical side of the relationship.

She'd experienced that sort of comradeship with Chuck to some extent and had assumed you could have either friendship or sex with a man, but not both. Daniel was demonstrating that she was wrong.

"Cute little town," Daniel said as they moved along Main Street at a snail's pace.

"You should see it at Christmas, with the white clapboard houses trimmed in evergreen and red bows, and little white lights everywhere." She was glad the slow pace had calmed St. Paddy. Or maybe emptying his bladder had done the trick. For whatever reason, he wasn't whining anymore.

"I'll bet it's also nice in the summer, when everything's in bloom," Daniel said.

"It is. And the best thing about it is the weekly paper."

"Because it carries your strip?"

"That's right."

Daniel nodded. "Sounds as if the people here have good

sense and a scenic location. Too bad they also run a speed trap."

"Luckily you're friends with the local gendarme."

"I guess you could say that. If we hadn't been friends, maybe he would have locked me up in addition to fining me."

"He wrote you a ticket?"

"Sure did. Apologized all over the place while he was doing it, too. Touching as hell. Just let old Timmy set foot in *my* town, though. I'll bust him for jaywalking."

Rose gazed at him. "I'd hoped once we got away from the city and our mothers that life would go a little smoother for us."

Daniel lapsed into a heavy brogue. "And so it has, lass. We're headed down the road to your wee cottage, and me mither's nowhere about creatin' a brouhaha, and neither is yours. Sure and 'tis a fine day, Rose Erin Kingsford."

She laughed, relieved to discover he wasn't really upset. Many men she'd known would have let a speeding ticket ruin their whole day. "How did you know my middle name?"

"Called a buddy in motor vehicles."

"Oh. Then you know about my—"

"Speeding tickets? My friend Timmy is an equal-opportunity ticketer, apparently. He told me you'd tried to show a little leg and get the fine reduced the first time around, but an upstanding officer such as himself can't be bought."

"I did not! Your *friend* has some nerve, saying that." She was all geared up to defend her integrity when she noticed the wide smile on his face. "He didn't say that at all. You made it up."

"Just so you know, you can try that sort of bribery with me anytime." He turned to her and waggled his eyebrows.

"So you can be had."

"Absolutely."

Warmth coursed through her. They were getting closer to her cottage, closer to being alone—truly, deliciously alone. Except for St. Paddy, of course.

"Time for you to navigate again," Daniel said. "We're almost through town."

Rose kept forgetting that Daniel hadn't been here before. She felt so comfortable with him that it seemed strange he hadn't been part of her life for a long time. "Take a right at the next stop sign, go over the bridge and take a left, then a right down the first lane. It's not marked."

"You weren't kidding about it being tucked away."

"That's what I looked for."

"You're planning to live here someday, aren't you?"

"Yes."

Daniel was silent for a while. "How soon?"

"My apartment lease expires in three months."

He stretched his arms against the wheel of the car. "Is that the time frame for us? Three months?"

The question hit her like a blow to the chest. "I...no, of course not. I wasn't thinking in those terms."

"What terms were you thinking in?"

"Daniel, I thought we weren't going to question the status of our relationship. I thought we were going to keep things loose, go with the feelings of the moment."

"That made a lot more sense when I thought you'd be living on the same island with me."

"My moving up here doesn't have to change anything. Not really. I can still drive down to the city. You can come up here."

He turned down the lane that wound its way to her cottage. "I guess you're right." He glanced at the pet carrier.

"I was wondering how you'd fit a full-grown Irish wolf-hound in your apartment. You weren't planning to try."

Guilt assailed her. He'd already made her feel as if she'd been hiding things from him, and she hadn't even broached the fatherhood issue. Her plan had seemed fine when it was on the drawing board, but now that she was trying to implement it, it seemed hopeless. Yet she couldn't bear to give up the idea of having a child. The urge had something to do with a strong mothering instinct and a lot to do with continuity. She was the only child of an only child. If she didn't carry on the line, no one else would. She blamed her Irish heritage for making that important to her.

But she'd begun to question the wisdom of asking Daniel to provide her with a baby. She'd only known him a short time, but she already suspected it might upset him. He had an ability to care deeply about people, and he might well hate the idea of fatherhood without all the usual connections. The same would probably be true of any man she considered worthy of the task. That was the fatal flaw in her reasoning, which she hadn't recognized until now.

They rounded a bend in the road and her little house came into view.

Daniel braked the car and stared. "It's an Irish cottage. Or at least it's the way I picture them. I've never actually been to Ireland."

"It's as close to an Irish cottage as I could get. I had the lace for the curtains shipped over, as well as one of those little fireplaces they use for burning peat, although I use wood."

"But that's a thatched roof. Nobody around here knows how to do that, do they?"

"It took me a long time, but I finally found somebody who'd emigrated just a few years ago. This was the first one he'd done in this country, but now he's gone into the business. He hadn't thought anybody would want to try it, but he's finding out it's turning into quite the rage."

Daniel put his foot on the brake as the car rolled into the driveway beside the cottage. Then he shut off the motor and studied the cottage a moment. At last he hooked an arm across the steering wheel and turned toward her. "It's perfect for you, Rose. If I hadn't guessed before that the place belonged to you, I would have once I'd seen it. This is where the creator of St. Paddy and Flynn should live."

"Thank you."

"I appreciate your bringing me up here. I can already tell it's a special place for you."

"You sound as if this will be the one and only time. I'm sure that we'll have many—"

He looked doubtful, a sad smile on his face.

"What?"

"I can see that you have a whole game plan mapped out, which you should, because you're loaded with talent. You're already somewhat rich and famous from your modeling. This next career will likely take you even further down that road."

"You don't know that's how it will go, and what if it does? We could still—"

"I may fit in your life all right now, Rose. But sooner or later, we'll move in different circles. Even if you don't realize it, I do."

"You're wrong. Very wrong."

St. Paddy began to whimper.

"We'd better get him in," Daniel said, reaching for his jacket.

As Rose opened the car door, she wondered why she should feel so bereft. Daniel had just outlined the course she'd hoped her life would take. Her strip would become famous, make her a lot of money, and she'd live quietly in this little cottage with her child. And without Daniel. The fame and fortune might not separate them, but her decision to have a baby out of wedlock would. What had seemed like the most idyllic existence she could imagine suddenly no longer held the same appeal.

Daniel took the pet carrier out of the car. "Come on, St. Paddy. You were born to live in this little thatched cottage."

Rose grabbed her coat and purse from the back seat and followed Daniel up the curved cobblestone walk. The flower beds lining the walk were covered in mulch, but in less than two months daffodils would trim the cobblestones in bands of yellow.

"I'll bet your mother loves this place," Daniel said as they approached the front door.

Rose dug her keys out of her purse. "She does. She helped me with everything—the landscaping, the antiques inside, the choice of colors. She said it was a bit like taking a trip back home." Rose stuck the key in the lock and turned.

"Has she ever been back to Ireland?"

"No. When she was married to my dad, he never seemed to have the time, and now that she's divorced, she doesn't want to go back and have to explain...everything." She paused before opening the door and glanced at him. "I suppose that sounds silly."

"Not to me. I grew up with that kind of conservative thinking, don't forget."

"I guess you did." She opened the door and motioned him inside. "Welcome to Rose of Tralee cottage." She followed him inside.

She'd wondered if he'd look out of place in the small cottage. To her surprise, he looked as if he belonged there, an Irish man who'd finally come home.

Perhaps it was because the antiques she'd chosen were rugged country pieces rather than delicate, spindly things. A hutch held pottery plates and bowls, and the trestle table in one corner was solid oak. The couch and rocking chair grouped in front of the stone hearth both looked plenty big enough to hold a man of Daniel's size. She'd chosen them with an active child and a big dog in mind. But the man standing in the middle of the room hadn't been part of the picture. Nevertheless, he fit it perfectly.

Daniel set down the pet carrier on the pine floor and surveyed the room.

"Do you like it?" she asked with some nervousness.

"I don't know a damn thing about decorating, but if I tried to imagine the perfect room, this would be it."

She couldn't keep the grin of satisfaction off her face. "I think so, too. When I'm in Manhattan and the pace is getting to me, I just close my eyes and picture myself here. It takes away all my stress."

St. Paddy pawed at the gate of his carrier.

"I guess we should let him out." Rose started over toward the carrier.

"I have a suggestion. Have you ever had a puppy before?"

"No. I wasn't allowed."

"Then I'm the voice of experience in this crowd. I've had two. And what I remember is that we confined them pretty much to the kitchen until they were paper trained. Otherwise…"

"I get the picture. But we can't close the door and keep him in there, away from us, all the time. That would be mean."

"If I remember right, we used a piece of board high enough that he couldn't get over it but low enough that we could step over it. We can make him a bed in the corner of the kitchen, and if you have a ticking alarm clock and a hot-water bottle, which sort of substitutes for the other puppies' warmth and heartbeat, we're in business.''

"I've heard about those things before. Do they really work?''

He grinned. "Sometimes. Sometimes the dog drives you crazy, like the breeder said.''

"I'm really glad you're here to help me with this puppy, Daniel. I might make a mess of things by myself.''

"I'm glad I'm here, too.'' His gaze caught and held hers for a moment. Then he looked away. "Do you have any scrap wood around?''

"There should be some in back left over from the renovations. If you'll go look, I'll get the windup clock out of the bedroom. I don't have a hot-water bottle, but I have one of those microwavable gel packs.''

"That'll work.''

She walked toward the bedroom and Daniel headed for the back door, which meant they had to pass each other.

As they did, he reached out an arm and spun her around to face him. "One for the road,'' he murmured, pulling her close.

Daniel's kiss, she discovered, could make her forget everything else. The velvet persuasion of his lips reminded her of all they had yet to share, and desire sluiced through her.

He ended the kiss just as she was getting started. She looked up at him, her knees weak, her brain fuzzy.

"Don't lose your place,'' he said, releasing her gently. "Right now we have to settle that puppy in.''

"What if he needs...lots of attention?'' For the first time she regretted her impulse.

"He's a baby. Babies sleep a lot, and he's definitely due for a nap.''

"Oh."

"And so am I." With a wink he was out the door.

Rose stood there for a full ten seconds before she was able to remember the errand she'd been about to run when he'd pulled her into his arms.

AN HOUR LATER Daniel had created the barrier across the kitchen doorway and unloaded the groceries from the car. Rose had found a cardboard box to serve as a dog bed and lined it with an old blanket from the linen closet. The clock and microwave pouch were tucked into the blanket. St. Paddy roamed the kitchen sniffing everything while Rose and Daniel watched him get acquainted with his new surroundings.

"How about newspapers?" Daniel asked.

"I'll get them." She stepped over the barrier and scooped up an armful from a basket next to the fireplace. Then she recrossed the barrier and started spreading the papers around the kitchen.

Daniel stooped down to help. "Are these local?"

"Yes." She laughed as St. Paddy tried to climb in her lap and nearly knocked her over.

"Did you take out the comic page?"

"Yes, but you just gave me an idea. I've got several extras." She handed him the rest of the newspapers. "I'm going to get one for St. Paddy."

"He may be big for his age, but I doubt he can read yet."

"It's symbolic. Be right back." Soon she returned with the comic page from a recent paper and laid it ceremoniously down in front of the puppy. "For you, m'lord."

St. Paddy looked down at the paper and back up at her, his tail wagging vigorously.

"See? He likes it," Rose said.

Daniel rolled his eyes. "He sure does. I think he wants you to read it to him."

"Why not?" She got down on her hands and knees, which the puppy acknowledged by licking her face. "Come on, Daniel. You read St. Paddy's speeches, and I'll be Flynn."

"Are you sure I'm right for the part? Don't you want me to audition first?"

"Just get down here and read, smart aleck. It was your idea."

Daniel sank to his knees beside her. "Here we have Daniel O'Malley, supercop, reading a comic strip to a dog." He placed both hands on the floor and went nose-to-nose with St. Paddy. "Do you realize what this could do to my tough-guy image if anybody found out, pup?"

St. Paddy responded by swiping a tongue over Daniel's nose.

"Tough guy, huh?" Rose chuckled.

"Criminals tremble at the mention of my name. Come here, you," Daniel said, wrapping one arm around the wriggling puppy. He adopted a thick brogue and started to read. St. Paddy grew still and cocked his head.

"Daniel, he's really listening," Rose whispered.

"Of course he is. Are you going to read your part or do I have to do everything around here?"

Rose read the words of the little leprechaun in a lilting, teasing voice.

Daniel glanced at her and grinned. "That's so cute."

She blushed, suddenly self-conscious. "It's just how I hear him in my head."

"I can tell." Still smiling, he returned his attention to the strip and read the next St. Paddy line.

She sensed he was watching her with that same smile on his face as she started to read her next line. She stopped halfway through. "Don't look at me. You're making me nervous."

"Nervous? With what you do for a living?"

"This is different."

"But you look so adorable when you start talking like Flynn."

"Don't look."

"Okay." He shielded St. Paddy's eyes. "Don't look, pup. She's shy."

Her color high, Rose continued reading in tandem with Daniel. When his rich laughter greeted her final line, she didn't think she'd ever felt so validated in her life. She gazed at him. "Thanks."

"I wouldn't have missed it for the world." He regarded her with an appreciative light in his eyes. "Ready to try and settle him in now?"

"Sure."

But Paddy didn't seem to want to stay in the box.

"Just sit on the floor by the box and keep petting him while he's in there. I'll bet he goes to sleep eventually," Daniel said. "In the meantime I'll make us a couple of sandwiches."

"I didn't even remember about lunch!"

"I'll bet you don't eat as much as I do, anyway. You're probably not very hungry."

"No, I'm not, but it still doesn't say much for my hostessing skills that I didn't even bring up the subject."

Daniel opened the refrigerator and pulled out lunch meat and lettuce. "I thought we agreed that I'd think about the food this weekend."

"And what am I supposed to think about?"

He shot her a quick grin. "Me."

As if she could help it. It might have seemed she had all her attention focused on the puppy curled up in the box, but she recorded every nuance as Daniel moved around the kitchen. She watched the way a lock of his dark hair fell on his forehead as he leaned over the counter to spread mustard on the bread. She noticed the way his jeans fit in the back as he walked over to pull a bag of chips out of the cupboard. When he came toward her, she noticed how they fit in the front, too.

If St. Paddy would only drift off to sleep, she'd suggest they refrigerate the sandwiches until later. But the puppy continued to gaze up at her with his soulful brown eyes. And she had, after all, just deprived him of his nine brothers and sisters. Getting this puppy right now might not have been the brightest move she'd ever made.

Daniel handed her half a sandwich. "Eat this. You'll need your strength."

"Is that right?" Remarks like that made her heart race, but she felt uncertain about letting him know just how far gone she was when it came to his considerable sex appeal. She took a bite of sandwich, which was very good.

He squatted down in front of her, part of a sandwich in his hand. "Yeah. I'm known as a regular love machine. Ask anybody."

"Hmm. A supercop and now a love machine." She took another bite, chewed and swallowed before addressing St. Paddy. "Tell me, my good man, have you heard the news of this man's prowess in the sack?"

St. Paddy looked up at her and opened his mouth in an enormous yawn.

Rose glanced at Daniel. "St. Paddy's unimpressed."

"He's a guy. Guys never want to admit someone is better at it than they are."

"And just how good are you?"

"Keep petting that puppy, who is definitely getting sleepy, and in about five minutes you'll find out."

"Oh, the experience lasts for that long, does it? The women must go wild over you."

"I meant in five minutes you'd *begin* to find out. I think I can manage a little more than five minutes' worth."

"I see." She took another bite of the sandwich, but it was merely for show. She couldn't taste it as she looked into his eyes.

"He's asleep," he murmured, taking the rest of her sandwich from her and putting it on the counter with his. "Take your hand away very, very slowly."

She eased her fingers away from the puppy's fur.

"I'm going to pull you to your feet. Just let me do the guiding, and you won't bump the box." He stood slowly and held out both hands.

Her gaze locked with his. She put her hands into his larger ones and he drew her slowly to her feet. By the time he'd pulled her upright, her heart was hammering with excitement.

"I'll back out of here. Just follow me."

With that glow of sensuality in his eyes, she would have followed him to Outer Mongolia. They moved cautiously over the barrier across the doorway of the kitchen.

Rose remembered the edge of the rag rug at the moment Daniel tripped on it and lost his balance. She tried to hold him upright, but he was far too heavy. They toppled backward, somehow managing to avoid the furniture, and landed on the floor with a heavy thud, Rose on top and Daniel on the bottom.

"Are you okay?" she asked, raising herself up to look down at him.

"Shh." He pulled her back to his chest. "Be still. Let's see if we woke him up."

"Oh, no doubt. Daniel, you probably hurt yourself. Let's—"

"I'm fine. Now be quiet. I think he's still asleep."

She rested her cheek against his chest and listened to the rapid thump of his heart through the fabric of his knit shirt. Slowly she reached up and unfastened a button on the placket at the neck.

"What do you think you're doing?"

"Checking to see if anything's broken." She slipped her hand inside his shirt.

His breathing quickened. "I've changed my mind. No telling what's wrong with me after that fall. I think you'd better check everything. Thoroughly."

9

DANIEL DIDN'T KID himself that this moment was the beginning of a long and glorious love affair. Rose needed someone right now, and thanks to his mother, he'd shown up. She was in transition between careers, between homes, between life-styles. Having someone to hold during a time like that could be a great comfort.

He'd hurt like hell when she no longer required his company. Yet knowing their time together was finite, he still gathered her close as they lay together on the braided rug and opened his heart. It was the only way he could make love to a woman, and Rose needed everything he could give her.

As Rose's hands crept beneath his shirt, he rolled her to her side and began kissing every freckle on her lovely Irish face. As he moved his lips over her warm skin, he hooked a finger in the tie holding her hair and pulled it down and away. He wanted her hair loose and wild, with its heady fragrance surrounding him as he nuzzled behind her ear.

He was glad he'd been interrupted back in her apartment. This was the place to make love to Rose, in this whitewashed cottage with its thatched roof and drifts of snowy lace at the leaded-glass windows. She tasted like the country, smelled like the country—fresh cream, wild honey, sparkling streams and grassy meadows. For a city boy, that was quite a treat. And Daniel feasted.

Her clothes came away with surprising ease as he uncovered more and more of the wonder that was Rose. Her skin seemed almost translucent, and her bones were so delicate that he was reminded of a Lladro porcelain figurine he'd broken as a child. Yet the heat pouring from her and the urgency of her touch told him she didn't want him to be gentle. He was gentle anyway. She had no idea of the brute strength in the hands of a well-trained cop, and she'd never find out from him.

Briefly, he thought of taking her into the bedroom so she'd have the softness of the mattress at her back, but then she unbuttoned the fly of his jeans and stroked him. He gave up the idea of moving anywhere as he became hard as a nightstick and crazy with the urge to bury himself inside her.

Gasping, he lifted his head to see if anything was handy that he could place beneath her. Two toss pillows were on the couch within arm's reach, and he grabbed them both. He tucked one under her head as he rolled her to her back and leaned down to explore her mouth once more. She'd worked her hand inside his briefs by this time, and he groaned with the intense pleasure. He would have to have her soon...very soon.

But first he wanted to take those saucy little breasts in his mouth. Their pert upward thrust enticed him far more than abundance would have, and the obvious sensitivity of her nipples as she whimpered and writhed beneath his ministrations converted him forever to the magic of small breasts.

He moved between her slender thighs and lifted her hips for the second pillow. As slight as she was, he might drive her right into the floor with the force of the desire building in him. He'd never before felt the blood roaring in his ears like this, or his hands trembling so much when he dug into his pocket for the condom he'd put there this morning.

It wasn't easy finding the condom and putting it on while he continued to kiss her mouth and caress her passion-slicked body. And her eyes—how he loved to slide his hand down between her thighs and watch the turbulent reaction in her green, green eyes. The way she lifted into his caress when he probed her moist channel told him he could bring her to climax that way, but he was too selfish. He wanted to be inside her when she felt the first explosion. He wanted those spasms to set off his own.

At last he managed to get the condom on. Braced above her, he fastened his gaze on hers and eased forward, stopping when he was just barely inside her. She made a sound low in her throat and grasped his hips, her whole body radiating impatience.

He resisted her urging. "We'll only have this moment once in our lives," he said.

Her voice was ragged with passion. "So you want it to take forever?"

He laughed. He didn't think he could laugh when he was worked up like this, but it turned out he could. "Yes." He leaned down and kissed her.

She nipped at his lower lip.

He lifted his head and gazed down at her. "You're a handful, Rose Kingsford."

"Then use both hands, Officer O'Malley."

So he did. He slipped one arm under her shoulders, holding her a little off the floor, and slid his other hand under her firm behind. Then, when he was quite sure he wouldn't slam her against the hard floor, he pushed deep.

She gasped.

He withdrew in concern. "Rose?"

"That was lovely," she said in a breathless whisper. "You come right back here, Daniel."

With a soft moan he came back, back to paradise, back

to the place it seemed he'd been seeking all his life. Nothing had ever seemed so right as locking his body tightly with hers, moving only enough to increase the delicious pressure for both of them. He'd wondered if he'd ever feel this perfection or if it was an impossible dream.

"Oh, Daniel," she murmured, her eyes closed and her voice full of awe. "Daniel."

"I'm here. Open your eyes, Rose."

Slowly her eyelids fluttered upward.

He looked into those green depths and saw more than momentary pleasure. In that moment he knew that Rose had opened her heart, as well. Perhaps she, like he, couldn't help herself.

"We're in trouble now," he whispered, gently increasing the rhythm.

"I know."

As the motion carried them both beyond reason, her body grew taut beneath his and her breathing came quick and fast. He focused on her face, suffused with desire and something more lasting than desire, and knew that he never wanted any other man to touch her like this, to possess either her body or her heart. Her violent climax triggered his, and at the moment of truth, her name was wrenched from him in an involuntary plea.

He *was* in trouble. Big trouble.

ROSE LAY in the tangle of clothes and wondered how in the heck she'd gotten herself in such a mess. For the first time in years she'd allowed a man to get under her skin. Daniel's sweetness and sense of humor had her questioning all her assumptions about marriage and happily-ever-afters. But this wasn't a very good time to be doing that now that she'd finally figured out what she wanted from life—a child, a new career and a charming country place to live in. A mounted policeman with the NYPD didn't fit in with any of that.

And as for Daniel, he'd been quite plain about his need for freedom. What it amounted to was that she'd picked a hell of a time to fall in love, and the worst person in the world to fall in love with.

Daniel's face was buried in her hair, but his weight didn't rest fully on her, so she knew he wasn't asleep. She ran her finger up his spine and felt the quiver of response. "I respect a man who can back up his boast," she murmured. "I haven't experienced the blanket, but you're heaven on a rug."

He stirred and nuzzled the side of her neck. "It helps to be holding paradise in my arms."

"Spoken like a true Irishman."

He raised up on one elbow and gazed down at her. "Go ahead. Make fun of what we just shared. Make fun of me. But I saw your eyes, and I know you're making jokes because you're scared to death."

She swallowed. "Okay, I'm scared. I've never felt anything quite like this."

He leaned down and brushed his lips against hers. "Doesn't fit into your scheme, does it?"

"Does it fit into yours?"

He hesitated. "No."

"What are we going to do?"

He lifted his head to look into her eyes. "I'm not sure yet. When the whole world shifts, a wise man gets his balance before he goes off in any direction."

She smiled. "Now that really sounds Irish."

"Must be the influence of this little cottage. I feel like John Wayne in *The Quiet Man*."

Rose wondered just how deeply he felt that role. John Wayne had played the part of a man who marries in that film. As she gazed into Daniel's dark eyes, she gradually became aware of another pair of brown eyes staring down at her in solemn wonder. She started to giggle.

Daniel looked puzzled and turned his head to follow the direction of her gaze.

St. Paddy licked his face.

"Yikes! Prison break."

"So much for your barrier theory."

"Keep an eye on him while I go wash up. We'll figure out something." He eased away from her, stood and walked unself-consciously into the bathroom.

Rose gazed after him. Sure enough, he had a small purple scar on his left buttock. He didn't seem the least worried about showing it off, either. She smiled to herself as she sat up to locate her underpants. While putting them on, she turned to St. Paddy, who was having a great time investigating the clothing scattered around the area. "Be a good dog," she said. "Don't—uh-oh."

St. Paddy scampered a short distance away with Daniel's briefs between his teeth.

"Come here," Rose coaxed.

The puppy edged forward, ready for a game.

"Just give them back." Easing forward, she made a grab for them and was instantly in a tug-of-war. "St. Paddy! Let go!"

The puppy tugged harder, his hind end in the air and his tail wagging madly.

Daniel walked in. "I need my—" he paused at the sound of ripping cotton "—duffel bag," he finished, going back to the bedroom.

"Daniel, I'm sorry," Rose called after him. "I'll buy you a new pair."

"Not on your life," he called back from the bedroom. "Those are my insurance policy against you telling anybody I read a comic strip to a dog. If you ever do, I'm telling the world you ripped my underwear in a fit of passion.''

"You wouldn't!"

"Just try me." He came back into the room wearing only a low-slung pair of navy briefs.

Rose looked him up and down and ran the tip of her tongue over her lips. "Is that an invitation, Officer O'Malley?"

He paused in the act of reaching for his jeans and glanced at her. Then he gave her a long, assessing look. "This is going to be some weekend," he said quietly.

Her heart beat faster. "I hope so."

"But first we'd better give that puppy some exercise so he'll sleep a long, long time."

"Good idea." She reveled in the promise contained in Daniel's intent gaze. "We'll take him for a walk."

THE WOODS surrounding the little cottage were soggy with the wet snowfall that had turned to rain at midday, so Rose decided to keep to the road when she and Daniel took St. Paddy for his first walk. She fashioned a makeshift collar out of a bandanna and found a length of clothesline for a temporary leash.

They stepped outside into the water-color light of a New England afternoon and Rose zipped up the ski jacket she kept at the cottage just for such walks in the woods. The pale sun touched oak and maple trees nubby with the promise of spring, and pine branches tipped light green with new growth.

Rose took a deep breath. "I love the way it smells here."

Daniel made a great show of filling his lungs. Then he began to cough.

Rose clapped him on the back. "Are you okay?"

"Sure." He cleared his throat and grinned at her. "I guess fresh air takes some getting used to, after a lifetime of car exhaust and rotting garbage."

Rose started down the road, with St. Paddy scampering around at the end of the clothesline. "Have you ever wanted to live in the country?" Instantly she regretted the impulsive question. Far too leading. And she didn't really want to lead anywhere.

"I guess *living* in the country never occurred to me, but I like the idea of vacations here." Daniel fell into step beside her on the asphalt lane. "I'm trained as a city cop, and I love the work."

It was the response she'd expected, yet still she felt disappointed. "I love the country. My mom says I have the heart of an Irish milkmaid."

"Don't tell me you're going to keep a cow in the backyard."

She laughed. "I've thought of it. Or a horse."

"Good God."

"What? You ride a horse on the job."

"Yeah, but he doesn't live in my apartment."

"Listen, don't pull that sophisticated-city-slicker routine with me, Daniel. I watched you with that animal, and you're crazy about him."

"Dan Foley's okay, I guess."

"Excuse me? What's his name?"

"Our horses are often named after an officer killed in the line of duty, and Lieutenant Dan Foley died during a drug bust about ten years ago. So that's my horse's name. It's a nice way of memorializing some of our heroes."

"How lovely and sentimental."

"Cops can be more sentimental than you might——uh-oh. Wildlife at two o'clock. Better hold that puppy."

Rose gripped the clothesline as a rabbit hopped across the road in front of them and St. Paddy leaped after it, pulling Rose slightly off balance. The rabbit disappeared into the underbrush as Rose coaxed St. Paddy back and got him headed in the same direction she and Daniel were walking.

"Judging from the size of those paws, you won't be able to haul him around like that much longer," Daniel said. "What did the breeder say? He'll gain a half pound a day?"

"Something like that."

"At that rate he'll outweigh you in no time."

"I suppose. But these dogs are bred for their good disposition. He'll just naturally want to please me."

"He's not the only one with that urge."

"Oh, really?" A shiver of pleasure travelled up her spine as she paused to glance at him. He looked as irresistibly masculine silhouetted against the darkening woods as he had inside her Irish cottage.

"Isn't it obvious?" A breeze ruffled his dark hair. "I figure I must look as eager as that pup."

"Think I could teach you to beg?"

"I think you already have." His gaze smoldered as he slipped a hand around her waist and drew her slowly toward him. "Kiss me, Rose."

"That's not begging." Her breath quickened as she moved into the magnetic force that surrounded him. "That's commanding."

"Please kiss me, then."

"In the middle of the road?"

"No, on my mouth. And give me the clothesline," he murmured, reaching for it. His body was warm and hard against hers. "If you forget what you're doing and turn that puppy loose, you'll never forgive me."

"What if *you* forget?"

"I'm a cop. I'm trained to do two things at once." Then his lips found hers.

She quickly realized she couldn't do two things at once, if one of them was kissing Daniel. Her response to him had always been quick, but now it was immediate. She moaned and wrapped her arms around his waist, pressing against the barrier of their clothing.

He lifted his mouth a fraction from hers. "I feel like tying this dog to a tree and dragging you into the woods."

Her heart was thudding so loud she could barely hear him. "It's muddy."

"I don't care." He nipped at her lower lip. "I don't care if we're both smeared with mud. In fact, I think I'd *like* rolling your tender body in the mud. There's something sexy about ooze."

The image fed the fever raging within her. If only he'd fill the aching void deep inside, she'd lie in the mud, in a pool of chocolate syrup, in a vat of whipped cream—

"Damn!" Daniel released her with a suddenness that made her stumble. He flung down the end of the rope he'd been holding and raced to the opposite end, which was still tied to the red bandanna lying in the road. St. Paddy had escaped.

10

ROSE'S STOMACH churned as she frantically scanned the woods bordering the road. No sign of a tan furry body anywhere. And she'd tied that knot so carefully, yet somehow he'd worked it loose, probably to go after another rabbit. She shouldn't have kissed Daniel, shouldn't have taken her eyes off that puppy for a minute.

"St. Paddy!" she called, a catch in her voice. "Oh, Daniel, he doesn't even know his name yet."

"That's okay." Daniel crossed to one side of the road and studied the underbrush. "Keep calling. Maybe he'll respond to the sound of your voice."

She gave silent thanks for his police skills, which had trained him to observe carefully. She kept calling.

He quickly crossed to the other side of the road and examined the verge. "He went this way," he said, striding through the mud, his boots making a sucking sound as he moved. "I can follow his paw prints, so this shouldn't be too tough. Maybe you should stay there, in case—"

"No chance, copper." Rose plunged after him, although her loafers didn't work quite as well as his boots and threatened to come off her feet with each step.

He glanced over his shoulder as he continued through the woods. "Rose, stay there."

"No."

"Okay, but watch your—"

"Look out!" she called, a millisecond before Daniel

tripped over a dead branch and fell headlong into the muck. She crouched down beside Daniel. "Are you okay?"

He pushed up on the palms of his hands and spit out a dead leaf. "Man, that was graceful. Don't you love the country?" His face was so covered with mud, he looked like a character in a minstrel show.

"You said there was something sexy about ooze."

"Thanks for reminding me of that. But I wasn't planning to throw myself facedown in it." He got to his feet and wiped the arm of his jacket across his eyes. Then he studied the ground again. "This way," he said, starting off.

Rose followed, nearly losing her shoes in the process.

Finally he crouched down in front of a large hollow log. "He's in there, I'll bet. Probably followed another rabbit."

Rose squatted down beside him so she could peer into the black opening. The loamy scent of plant decay mingled with what she thought might be the smell of wet dog. "St. Paddy," she called softly. "Come here, little guy. You're too young to be out in the woods alone."

No answer.

Rose's stomach twisted with anxiety. "I hope something didn't get him in there."

"Whatever would fit in this log isn't any bigger than he is, and from the look of his prints, he crawled in under his own steam. He probably just got tired and fell asleep. Let me see what happens when I reach inside."

"Yuck. Think of what could be in there."

"Country stuff." He grinned at her. "Country reality, as opposed to country fantasy."

"You're making fun of me."

"Gently, very gently. There's still some city girl in you, Rose." He dropped to his knees beside the hollow log.

"Daniel, you're going to get—"

"Muddy?" He wriggled down until his chest was on the ground before easing his hand into the log. "Now that would be a real shame, wouldn't it?"

Rose sighed. "Disasters seem to happen to you whenever you're around me."

"I'm not complaining."

"I can't imagine why not."

"Think of the fun we'll have cleaning up." He shoved his arm in a little farther. "Hey, pup. Come on out."

"Can you reach him?"

"Can't seem to. Wish my arm was a little longer. Damn, where's a superhero when you need him?"

Rose gazed at him lying in the mud, heedless of his own discomfort as he reached deep into the hollow log. "I'd say I have one," she said softly.

"Oh, sure." He grunted as he tried to get his arm in more. "I'm the guy who demanded a kiss when we both should have been watching the dog."

"I'm the one who didn't tie the bandanna knot tight enough," Rose said. "I don't want you blaming yourself."

Daniel began to chuckle.

"What's so funny?"

"Something's licking my fingers. I sure hope it's your puppy."

"It has to be him! Can you grab him?"

"Not unless you want me to pull him out by his tongue."

"Daniel," she said, her voice rising in excitement, "just move your hand back gradually. Maybe he'll keep licking your fingers and follow your hand right out."

"He just might. Did anyone ever tell you that you're very smart?"

"Thank you. It's not usually the first thing men notice about me."

"Can't blame them for that, Rose." He slowly eased his arm out of the hollow log. "You're very beautiful."

"Which doesn't necessarily lead to happiness."

"You sound as if it's a disadvantage, being beautiful."

"In some ways it is."

"I'd like to debate that with you later. Okay, get ready. Lean over me and when he sticks his head out, grab him by the scruff of his neck like you did in the car."

Rose positioned herself above him. "I'll be forever in your debt for this, Daniel."

"And don't think I won't collect."

Mud and all, his nearness turned her on. "That sounds very promising."

"And you'd better stop whispering sweet nothings in my ear or I'm liable to screw this up."

"Right." She tried to empty all sensual thoughts of Daniel from her mind as she concentrated on the opening where his hand was now buried only up to the wrist. Gradually he drew his fingers out.

Sure enough, a pink tongue and a stubby snout followed. Rose waited until St. Paddy's floppy ears cleared the ragged edge of the log before she pounced, grabbing a fistful of dog. St. Paddy squealed in surprise and wiggled in her grip. She wrapped both arms around him, lost her balance and fell backwards into a tangle of bushes. But she kept her hold on the dog.

Daniel eased himself up and sat back on his heels. "Why, Rose, you're sitting in a bush."

She hugged the squirming puppy to her chest. "If you say that must make it a Rose bush, I'll never speak to you again."

"Wouldn't dream of saying that. Want some help with that critter?"

"Please."

He got to his feet and leaned down. "Let me take him so you can climb out of there."

She maintained a firm hold on the scruff of St. Paddy's neck while Daniel gathered the dog into his arms. "Got him?"

"Got him."

He lifted the thirty-five-pound animal without effort. After he backed away she extricated herself, ripping the back pocket of her designer jeans in the process.

Muttering to herself, she finally glanced up to see Daniel cradling St. Paddy as he might a toddler and speaking to him in a low, soothing voice. For a moment she stood transfixed by the sight of Daniel comforting the dog. *He would make a wonderful father*, whispered a voice in the back of her mind. If she ever considered trusting a man for the long haul, it would be a man like Daniel. But the timing was way off. He wasn't ready for a wife, and she was more than ready for a child. Nothing about their lives fit together.

Daniel glanced up at her and smiled. "I think he's fine."

That smile found its way into her heart. She could feel it bury itself deep and knew she'd remember the way he looked at this moment—muddy, triumphant and very sexy—for the rest of her life.

"Let's go home," she said.

THANK GOD the dog episode had turned out okay, Daniel thought. He held St. Paddy while he and Rose stood just inside the back door of her cottage. There she subjected him to the sweet torture of watching her peel off her muddy clothes while his hands were completely occupied hanging on to the squirming puppy.

In a way it was fortunate that he couldn't touch her and interfere with her graceful movements as she undressed. Rose had refined the process into performance art, and he felt privileged to be able to enjoy the show. His mouth grew moist and his erection strained against the fly of mud-caked jeans when she stripped down to nothing but her French-cut briefs.

Once her muddy clothes were off, she went in search of an old blanket to wrap around St. Paddy. She returned with it and sat on the floor with the blanket-wrapped dog while Daniel stripped down to his briefs. Then he carried the dog while she walked ahead of him and started the water running in the claw-footed tub.

"I want to make sure he doesn't scratch you," he said as he carefully lowered St. Paddy into the water.

She gave him an elfin grin. "Don't worry. I don't have any swimsuit sessions coming up soon. A little scratch won't ruin my career."

He glanced at her alabaster skin dusted with freckles. "I wasn't thinking of your career. I was thinking it would be a crime to mar skin like that for any reason."

Her smile faded. "See, that's what I mean. Men always expect perfection of someone like me."

"I don't expect perfection. I just—" He was prevented from continuing the explanation as St. Paddy started to climb out of the tub and it took both of them to keep the slippery dog inside. "Let me hold while you wash him," Daniel said.

She glanced sideways at him through a tangle of coppery curls. "Okay. Listen, I'm sorry I snapped at you."

Daniel leaned over the tub and got a firm hold of St. Paddy's chest and hind end. "You're forgiven." Shoulder to bare shoulder like this, he'd have forgiven her much worse transgressions, but he didn't want to let the subject drop, either. "Apparently you've been dating a string of men who only care about what you look like, but you've just come to the end of that run. If beauty was the only attraction, I wouldn't be here."

Rose used a washcloth on the puppy's face. "Then why do I get the feeling I'm like a new car and you're afraid to damage the paint job?"

His answering chuckle was rueful. "Good comparison. Maybe I do feel that way a little. I've never been with someone so..."

"Perfect? Believe me, I'm not."

"Okay, not perfect, but incredibly fragile and delicate." The puppy tried to get away and he tightened his grip. "Whatever that quality is that's made you a successful model. It's intimidating as hell when you get up close and personal with someone who reminds you of fine china."

"I don't want to be treated like fine china!" She scrubbed the washcloth across St. Paddy's back.

"You want rough sex?"

"No. For heaven's sake!"

"Okay, I get your point. You want to be treated like a flesh-and-blood woman."

"Exactly."

"You missed a glob of dirt on his back leg. There. That's it." Her nipple brushed his arm and he fought the urge to let go of the puppy and take an armful of Rose. The cotton of his briefs stirred with the beginnings of an erection.

"I think it's time I had an honest-to-goodness hickey."

Damn, but she had a way with words. "This isn't the best time to announce intentions like that."

"Why not? We're both nearly naked."

"Really? I hadn't noticed."

"We'll be done washing St. Paddy in a minute. I've never had a hickey, Daniel," she persisted earnestly as she continued to wash the quivering pup. "If you gave me a hickey you'd get over this thing about my being so delicate and perfect. You were so afraid I'd get bruised when we made love on the floor."

"How do you know?"

"All those pillows, and holding me the way you did. I could tell."

A ferocious ache gripped him as he remembered just what that session on the floor had been like. "Let's change the subject."

"I think I'd like a hickey on my bottom, in the same place you have that sexy bullet scar of yours."

"What do you know about a bullet scar?"

"Your mother told me about it in the tearoom. She said it made you shy around women, which was why you weren't married. She thought I could get you over that self-consciousness about a scar on your...bum, as she said."

"Dear God."

She glanced slyly down at his briefs. "I think I have, from the looks of things."

"You little tease. You're talking this way on purpose to drive me crazy, aren't you?"

"Is it working?"

He gave her a searing look. "Get a towel for this pup."

He toweled St. Paddy off in record time and carried him into the kitchen.

"Y'all come back," Rose called after him.

"Count on it." Daniel took St. Paddy into the kitchen, and once the puppy was tucked into his box he drifted right off to sleep. Daniel figured the puppy would sleep for a while, maybe long enough to give Daniel some privacy with Rose. It was time for him to prove to her that he didn't consider her to be made of porcelain.

He washed his face and hands in the kitchen sink and dried off with a paper towel. When he returned to the bathroom she'd cleaned out the tub and was running fresh water in it.

She was leaning both hands on the tub, her legs braced slightly apart as she glanced over her shoulder. "Is he asleep?"

The pose was so provocative his mouth went dry. "Out...out like a light."

"You can have first bath."

"I think we'll do this together."

She looked him up and down, excitement lighting her eyes. "I don't know if we'll both fit, officer. You seem to have grown."

"We'll work on it." He slipped off his briefs, releasing a full erection, and walked toward her. Her quick intake of breath and a darkening of her eyes were his reward. Holding her gaze he slid two fingers under the delicate lace panel inset of her panties, and in one swift motion ripped the garment from her body. He was through being tentative.

"Daniel!"

"You can tell people I ripped them in a fit of passion." He stepped into the tub and offered her his hand. Wordlessly she stepped in after him as warm water swirled around their ankles. "Turn around," he said.

Her eyes widened, but she turned her back to him.

Taking the curved bar of soap from the holder beside the tub, he knelt in the water behind her, dampened the soap and eased the bar up the back of her leg. She quivered. He dipped the bar in the water again and ran it slowly up the back of her other leg to the top of her thigh. Then he cupped his hand, scooped up warm water and allowed it to trickle down her thigh.

"What are you doing?" she murmured, her voice breathy.

"Cleaning you up." He soaped between her thighs with lazy circular strokes before rinsing with more cupped water.

"I've never had...a bath like this."

"It gets better." He paused briefly to turn off the tap. Then he washed the curve of her backside slowly while he reveled in the way her breathing grew faster and more shallow. He wondered if she'd eventually be so in tune with him that she'd climax with only this kind of caress. He wondered if he'd be her lover long enough to find out.

The soap had become slippery, so he tightened his grip when he slid it between the petals of her femininity. As the curve of the bar came in contact with her flash point, she gasped. He wrapped an arm around her waist to hold her steady as he rubbed the soap back and forth. Then he tossed the soap aside and began to rinse her with splashes of water, followed by intimate explorations with his fingers.

Her legs began to shake. "Daniel—"

"I've got you. Go with it, Rose."

Continuing the caress, he began kissing the tender flesh of her backside. The kisses progressed to gentle nips as she moaned and trembled in the circle of his arm. When she cried out with the first convulsion of her orgasm, he placed his mouth on the exact spot she'd requested and applied firm suction. If nothing else, she'd have a bruise to remember him by.

Perhaps it was her long moan of completion, or the act of marking her, or her stance when he'd first come back into the room, but a primitive lust took command of him, a driving need he could not control. He'd never intended to make love to her in the bathtub, because he hadn't prepared for it, but he was no longer rational.

Desperate to have her in a way that harkened back to the most basic needs of a man for a woman, he got to his feet and leaned her forward over his arm. Once her hands were braced on the edge of the tub, he grasped her hips and entered her, pushing deep. He never remembered such blinding passion. It seemed that burying himself inside her was absolutely necessary, and without this release he would surely die. His strokes were swift, his climax indescribable.

As the red haze slowly cleared, he was swamped by feelings of tenderness...and regret. He had no right to act without a thought for consequences. Withdrawing gently, he kept his arm around her as he stepped from the tub and grabbed an oversize bath towel. He wrapped her in it and lifted her out of the tub to set her on the bath mat.

"Wow," she said, her voice husky.

"Yeah." And now they had to discuss the possible consequences, he thought. But he postponed it, wanting to maintain the soft joy that surrounded them in the aftermath of raw passion satisfied. He dried her carefully, crouching down to run the towel over her legs and buttocks. Sure enough, a definite bruise about the size of a silver dollar was forming there.

"You gave me a hickey, didn't you?"

"Yep." And he figured placing that brand on her was probably what had stirred the instinct passed down by his ancient forebears to complete the possession.

"Hold that hand mirror behind me so I can see."

He took the gilt-framed mirror from the counter and held it while she peered over her shoulder at the round, purple mark.

"Looks like an expert job."

"You came to the master." He stood and put the mirror back on the counter.

"Don't laugh, but I really like it. It's like a badge of womanhood. Now I have another request. Am I too big for you to carry into the bedroom?"

He smiled at her. "Depends on how you want to be carried."

"What do you mean?"

"I can manage it this way." He grasped her arm, stooped and hoisted her over his shoulder.

"Hey! That's not romantic."

"But it gets the job done." Laughing, he hauled her into the bedroom and dumped her onto the feather bed with its bank of lace-trimmed pillows scattered over the headboard. "And in my line of work, that's the main goal. It doesn't have to be pretty."

"I swear you have been taking lessons from old John Wayne movies."

He looked at her lying there amidst the white lace and wanted her again. But the time had come to confront the realities of nature. He climbed in beside her and took her into his arms. "We need to talk, Rose."

She snuggled against him. "What a novel suggestion."

"Hey, this is serious stuff." He shifted her so he could look into her eyes. "I lost control. We need to face what might happen as a result."

Her gaze was warm. "Don't take all the blame on yourself. I could have stopped you."

"Maybe not."

Her eyebrows lifted. "If I'd said no, you would have forced me?"

"No." He gave her a lazy grin. "I would have convinced you to say yes."

"Oh, ho! I guess I don't have to worry about damaging your ego."

"We're talking about desperation, not ego. I've never felt quite so…needy as I did then." He was admitting quite a bit with that statement. He searched her face to see how she'd react to it.

"Neither have I," she said, her expression open and vulnerable.

He took a deep breath and decided to risk a little more. "When I agreed to this weekend, I thought we'd have a fling, a fun roll in the hay, with no complications. It's what we both said we wanted." He paused. "But this doesn't feel like a fling."

"No, it doesn't feel that way to me, either."

He leaned down and pressed his lips gently to hers. "Thank you for saying that," he murmured, kissing the freckles on the bridge of her nose. "But even if we're both rethinking the situation, from now on we're using protection. We don't need the added pressure of an accident right now."

"True, and I can't be trusted to be the voice of reason, obviously. I didn't want to stop, either."

His blood began to heat anew. He sat up and swung his legs off the bed. "And it's obvious that we're headed down that road again. I'm going for supplies."

"Good idea. But really, Daniel, I don't think we have to worry. Getting pregnant with one slipup is unusual, don't you think?"

He stood. "Not so unusual for an Irishman."

11

MAUREEN O'MALLEY wished that Daniel hadn't gone off to his training session on this particular weekend. The parish was having a special Friday night potluck, and she'd figured on talking Daniel into going because she knew he had the time off. At least three young Irish ladies would be there that Maureen wanted Daniel to meet, now that Rose Kingsford had turned out to be such a disaster.

Maureen was putting the final touches on her chowder casserole when the phone rang. Thinking it was Fran Kavanagh, who'd suggested sharing a cab to the church in view of the weather, Maureen dried her hands on her apron, hurried to the phone and answered it slightly out of breath.

"You're panting as if you'd run all the way to the phone. Were you expecting a gentleman caller, Maureen Fiona?"

"*You!*" Once she recognized Bridget's voice, Maureen slammed down the receiver.

It rang again.

Maureen snatched it up. "I'll not be talking to you." She started to hang up again.

"It's about Daniel!" yelled Bridget.

Fear twisted Maureen's insides as she pressed the receiver to her ear. "What about him? Is he all right?"

"Physically, I'm sure he's fine. But his soul is in terrible danger."

Maureen let her breath out in a whoosh of sound. "Well, I care about his soul, naturally, but his body is my first concern. 'Tis just like you, Bridget Hogan, scaring a person half to death. I thought there'd been an accident or the like."

"There well could be if we don't put a stop to what's going on," Bridget said darkly.

"You always were one to drag out a story. As Daniel says, cut to the chase."

A mighty sigh carried across the telephone line. "This isn't easy for me to say about my own flesh and blood. My daughter, Rose—"

"I know perfectly well who your daughter is, you deceitful old banshee!"

"I'm the same age as you! And look twenty times better, too!"

"Ha! You know what happens when you're skinny and you get old? Sag, sag, sag! As my mother used to say, 'After fifty, plump up and stay seated.'"

"Never mind what your mother used to say. What I'm trying to tell you, if you'll be still for one second, is that Rose wants to have a child out of wedlock."

"No!"

"Yes. On purpose, and raise the baby all by herself. I don't know where she got such an idea."

"If you don't know, I do. 'Tis because you married a Protestant Brit instead of a good Irish Catholic, and that's the truth of it."

"Cecil has nothing to do with this idea of hers." There was a pause. "No, come to think of it, he probably *is* to blame. I'm glad you mentioned it. But that doesn't matter now. We have to stop them."

"Them?" Maureen had a sick feeling she knew what was coming.

"She's picked your Daniel as the father for this unholy plan."

"He wouldn't be doin' such a thing!"

"What if he doesn't know? What if she puts one over on him?"

"If she tricks Daniel into getting her in the family way, I will wring her neck for her! Good thing he's off on a training weekend with the department."

"You really think that's where he is, you silly goose?"

Maureen drew herself up to her full height of five feet, two inches. "He wouldn't be lying to his own mother."

"Rose lied to me. I finally weaseled it out of her agency that she's on holiday this weekend, not on assignment as she told me."

"We've already established Rose's character. 'Tis not surprising that she lied to you."

"I wouldn't be casting stones, if I were you, until you call your son's station," Bridget challenged. "See if there is a training weekend or not."

"I won't."

"I know you, Maureen, and you will, as soon as I hang up. You'd better take down my number so you can call me back and we can figure out what to do."

"I won't be calling, because Daniel's on a training weekend."

"You'll call me back, all right." Bridget recited her number.

Maureen squeezed her eyes shut and started to hum, as if she didn't need that number any more than a second set of thumbs. "Goodbye, Bridget. I'll not be speaking to you again in this lifetime." She hung up the phone.

Five minutes later she was obliged to dial Bridget's number, which had stuck in her mind like glue. "Where do you think they went?'' she asked without identifying herself.

"Oh, and who would *this* be?'' Bridget asked.

"You well know who 'tis.''

"Could this be the mother of that boy who would never lie?''

"Bridget Mary, you haven't changed a bit! Are you going to tell me where you think they went, or must I come over there and sit on you until you decide to be nice?''

"I know exactly where they went. Rose has a little cottage about two hours north of the city.''

Maureen gasped. "They're shacked up?''

"Honestly, get with it. Nobody says 'shacked up' these days. Anyway, we have to go up there. Do you have a car?''

Maureen thought of her husband's old Pontiac parked in the apartment house's basement garage. Daniel had been trying to get her to sell it, but she couldn't bring herself to do that. She hadn't told Daniel, but sometimes she went down to the garage and just sat in the passenger seat, pretending she and Patrick were about to take a drive.

"Goodness, woman, do you have a car or not? Or am I right in supposing you're losing your marbles?''

"'Tis my husband's car.''

"Can you drive it?''

Maureen thought about the few solo trips she'd made in the big old Pontiac. She remembered a wee problem with backing and cornering. But she wasn't about to tell Bridget about that and let her get the upper hand. "Yes, I can,'' she said.

"Good. Come over and pick me up.''

Maureen panicked and grabbed the first excuse she could think of. "But 'twill be getting on toward dark in another hour or so. We can't be gallivanting around upstate in the dark, Bridget.''

Indistinct muttering greeted that announcement.

''What's that you're saying?'' Maureen asked.

''The deed will be done by then!'' she hissed. ''But it can't be helped. They probably fell to it once they arrived, so we'd already be too late, and I suppose we shouldn't go at night. All we have left is to confront them and make certain they do the honorable thing.''

''Get married?'' Maureen squeaked.

''It's a black day, isn't it? When you and I have to contemplate becoming related, I mean. Can't be helped. Pick me up at eight. Here's the address.''

Maureen wrote down the address on the back of the electric bill. A Central Park West address. She'd have to drive into the heart of Manhattan. She hung up the phone and crossed herself.

ST. PADDY SLEPT for two hours, allowing his new owner to enjoy a gloriously long lovemaking session on the feather bed with Daniel, and to share a simple meal with him in front of the small fireplace. They'd found they both liked sitting on the floor next to the rustic coffee table.

Daniel had braced a chair against the board barricading Paddy inside the kitchen. They'd found Paddy was strong enough to push the heavy board aside and wiggle out the opening.

They'd just poured another glass of wine and started a game of chess when the puppy scratched at the board. Rose let him out, tied the bandanna collar around his neck, knotting it tighter this time, and took him outside briefly while Daniel stoked up the fire.

After Rose fed the puppy, she decided to let him stay

in the living room while she and Daniel finished their chess game.

St. Paddy roamed the living room for a few seconds before flopping down next to Daniel and attacking his shoe.

"Paddy, no!" Rose started to get up and pull him away.

"It's okay. He's just teething and needs something to chew."

"I have some old loafers in the closet that I was planning to give away."

"No, then he'll learn to chew up shoes. A few rags knotted together would be better."

"Let me see what I can find." Rose rummaged through the laundry area and came up with some likely candidates. She brought them to Daniel, who tied them into a chew toy for St. Paddy.

The puppy flopped down and started working away at the knotted rags.

Rose resumed her seat on the floor and studied her next chess move. "You seem to know a lot about dogs," she said after moving her knight.

"As I said, we had family pets when I was growing up." Daniel captured her knight with his pawn.

"Don't you miss that companionship?" She captured his knight with her bishop.

"Pets don't fit the bachelor existence too well." He moved his queen out of danger.

Rose gazed at him. "So you picked a job where you ride a horse."

He shrugged. "Just following in my dad's footsteps."

"You know what I think? I think you'd have a great time in the country, playing with all the animals." She moved her bishop again. "Check."

He leaned his elbows on his knees and looked at her.

"Going back to something you said today, is that an invitation?"

She forgot about the chess game. "Do you want it to be?"

He sighed and ran his fingers through his hair. "I don't know, Rose. All this—" His gesture encompassed the fire, the puppy, and her. "It's very appealing. But I couldn't afford something like this on my salary."

"Oh, for heaven's sake! What difference does it make who earns the money?"

His mouth quirked. "In my world, it makes a hell of a lot of difference."

"Then your world is somewhere back in the nineteenth century. Am I to be punished because my career pays better than yours? Are you going to deny me your company because modeling is valued more highly than peacekeeping? Which is ludicrous, by the way, but it's how society works these days."

"You're asking me to go back on decades of indoctrination if I allow a woman to foot the bill."

She could tell he was only half joking. "Well, I won't give up this cottage and toss my investments in the ocean to satisfy your male ego. So, if you want me, you have to accept my money."

"Love me, love my portfolio?"

Her breath caught at his use of the word, even so casually. She tried to maintain the same tone, but didn't quite pull it off. "I guess so." Her voice quavered just a little.

He set down his wineglass. "Rose, I—"

St. Paddy jumped up and knocked the edge of the chessboard, scattering the pieces.

"Hey, you," Daniel said, grabbing the puppy and falling to the floor with him. "I was all set to win that game until you butted in."

"Likely story," Rose said. "You knew you were going to lose, so you pinched him and made him bump the board." But it wasn't the destruction of the chess game that disappointed her. She wanted to know what Daniel had been about to say before St. Paddy got into the act. Had he been about to broach the subject of a commitment? Neither of them had wanted that at the beginning, but they hadn't realized how strong and how quickly the bond would develop between them. She'd abandoned the idea of asking him to father her child, but a new, more exciting prospect was presenting itself. Perhaps she could have a child *and* Daniel.

He was reaching out to her, but tentatively. The relationship was still fragile, and a telling moment had just been interrupted by her puppy. She couldn't blame St. Paddy. He hadn't asked to be part of this weekend. But as she watched Daniel roll on the floor with the dog, she realized that she was seeing a side of this New York cop she'd never have known otherwise. Daniel had that rare combination of sensuality and tenderness that she'd dreamed of but never found.

Daniel straightened and set St. Paddy firmly on the floor. Then he quieted him by stroking his back. As he caressed the dog, he picked up his wine and drained it.

"You looked as if you were really having fun with him," Rose said.

"On a scale of one to ten, wrestling with a dog on the floor is about a seven. Fun, but not outstanding."

"Really?" She knew she was blatantly fishing and didn't even care. "What's better?"

"Galloping Dan Foley through the streets of New York, which I don't get to do very often, by the way, would be at least a nine."

"Then what's a ten?" She hoped she knew the answer.

"I took a parachute-jumping course once. Leaping from a plane at twelve thousand feet would have to rate a ten."

"Oh." She looked into the glowing embers of the fireplace.

"Rose?"

She glanced back at him.

"Making love to you is off the charts," he said with a smile. "I can't count that high."

"Oh." This time the exclamation came out as a breathy whisper.

"And it's been a long time since we've made love."

Her nerve endings sizzled. "More than three hours."

He stood and held out both hands. "Let's not make it four." When she placed her hands in his, he pulled her to her feet and into his arms.

Much as she longed to walk straight into the bedroom with him, she couldn't ignore her new responsibility. "I should put St. Paddy in the kitchen."

He kissed her swiftly and firmly. "I'll do it. Go in and get that feather bed warm."

After going into the bedroom, Rose turned on the Tiffany bedside lamp and undressed quickly. On impulse, she took a decorative carafe of lavender water from the bedside table and sprinkled a few drops on the sheets and pillowcases. Then she climbed between the sheets, nestled against the cloud-soft mattress, and closed her eyes, a smile of anticipation on her face.

Her eyes snapped open and her smile faded as she suddenly realized what she'd done to herself. She'd never lie here again without thinking of Daniel. She'd never lie here again without *wanting* Daniel. Her hideaway would no longer beckon with the same promise, unless Daniel was part of the picture, but she still didn't know if he was interested in sharing her dream. She'd just thrown a major spanner into the works of her master plan.

The embodiment of that spanner walked through the bedroom door and stripped off his shirt. For the life of her she could summon up no regret, and not just because Daniel was magnificent to look at. When he held her in an embrace both strong and tender, she felt cherished. In her limited experience with physical love, she'd been leered at, fondled and even admired, as one would admire an inanimate object. Daniel was the first man who had ever cherished her.

"Is St. Paddy okay?" she asked.

"He's asleep. The ticking clock seems to be working."

"Good." Hot desire flowed through her as he undressed and she thought of the pleasure to follow.

He discarded the last of his clothes and slipped into bed beside her. "Heaven couldn't be any better than this," he murmured, gathering her close. "It even smells like heaven."

"Lavender water." She molded herself to his virile body.

"Nope." He nuzzled behind her ear. "Eau de Rosie."

"Nobody calls me Rosie."

"Somebody does now." He kissed the tip of her breast. "Touch me, Rosie. Touch me where it counts."

She did, grasping his heated shaft and caressing him until he moaned and pulled her hand away.

"You'd better stop, or I'll finish this before we really start," he said in a husky voice as he reached for the condom on the bedside table.

"Just following instructions, Officer."

"Oh, that's right." He snugged the condom into place and moved over her. "You once said my cop voice was intimidating."

"Extremely."

His dark gaze burned with need, and a fine sheen of sweat covered his shoulders. "So if I give you orders, you'll follow them?"

"I can't seem to help myself."

"A man could ask for no more." He leaned down and nibbled at her lower lip. "Spread your legs, Rosie, girl," he whispered. "And rise to meet me, lass."

She didn't need orders to welcome him deep inside her. Instinct drove her to this melding of bodies, and she suspected a melding of hearts, as well. When they were well and truly locked together, she wrapped her arms around him and looked up into his eyes. "Any more orders?"

"Just one."

She held her breath. From the intensity of his expression, he was in the grip of a forceful emotion.

"Love me."

Her response came without hesitation. "Yes."

He closed his eyes and took a shuddering breath. Then he opened them and gazed down at her. "I won't get in your way, Rose."

"Maybe I want you in my way, you hardheaded Irishman."

A soft smile touched his mouth as he began to move slowly within her. "I'll need convincing."

Her body tightened another notch with each stroke. "How?"

"By making love to me about a million times."

12

DANIEL FOUND his heart was too full for sleep, so he lay in a half-conscious daze of pleasure, his arms filled with the most wonderful woman in the world. He knew he and Rose had some problems to work out if they were seriously considering a permanent relationship. He'd found the woman worth giving up the mounted patrol for, but he wasn't ready to quit the force completely, and Rose had her heart set on this little cottage in the woods. The cottage was a hell of a long way from the city and the life he was used to.

Of course, this cottage had the advantage of also being far away from both of their mothers. God, he didn't even want to think about their reaction if he and Rose made an announcement. They'd have to hold the wedding in shifts, one for Maureen and the second for Bridget.

The wedding. The concept of matrimony had once been unacceptable, and now he couldn't imagine an alternative. Rose was everything he'd always wanted—intelligent, creative, caring and sexy. Not to mention the charisma that made her unique, the charisma that had ensnared him, heart and soul.

He was so engrossed in his thoughts that it took him awhile to hear the whimpering from the kitchen.

Rose stirred and hugged him closer. "St. Paddy's unhappy in there."

"Afraid so."

"He sounds pitiful, Daniel."

"I know. But remember what the breeder said. We have to tough it out."

"You're right. I'm sure he'll stop soon."

Daniel stroked her hair as they lay together and listened to St. Paddy cry. The sound tore at his heart. He thought of how the puppy must have spent the previous night snuggled with his litter mates and his barnyard friends. Now he was completely alone. Frightened. Unable to understand why he was cut off from all love and attention.

"I'm not good at this, Rosie," Daniel admitted.

"Neither am I."

Finally he sat up with a muttered oath. "You'd have to be a sociopath to be good at this. I'm getting him."

"Daniel, is this a good idea? A half pound a day, remember. The breeder said taking him to bed would be like trying to eat one potato chip out of the bag."

"We'll bring his box in and have him sleep in that. It's his first night, and he has to be scared to death." He headed for the kitchen.

Flipping on the kitchen light, he blinked in the glare. St. Paddy was standing right next to the board looking pathetically eager to see him. Daniel opened the makeshift gate, walked over and picked up the cardboard box.

"Just for tonight," he said in his sternest cop voice as he led the puppy, dancing in ecstasy, back to the bedroom.

He positioned the box next to the bed and lifted the puppy into it before climbing back into bed beside Rose. "There," he said, gathering her close.

St. Paddy began to whine and Rose began to laugh.

Daniel released her and rolled over to address the puppy, who by now had his feet on the edge of the mattress. "Lie down and go to sleep."

Rose continued to laugh.

"Don't pay attention to her. She doesn't respect my authority, but I expect you to. Now get down, Paddy." The puppy leaned forward and swiped a tongue over Daniel's nose.

Rose peered over Daniel's shoulder. "Oh, look at him. Poor thing. He wants to sleep with us."

"He's staying in his box."

St. Paddy rested his head between his paws and gazed up at them.

"Aw, Daniel. Doesn't that just melt your heart?"

"He's a con man, Rose, and he has you all figured out. He knows if he gives you that look, you'll let him do anything he wants."

She ran a foot along his calf. "You're the one who let him out."

"And it'll work fine as long as he learns to sleep in his box."

"But look at that face."

Daniel rolled over toward her. "I'm ignoring him. He's staying in the box, Rose."

St. Paddy let out a long, heartfelt sigh.

Daniel lay staring into Rose's eyes as Paddy sighed again, this time with more gusto.

"Daniel."

"No, Rose."

Then the bed began to wiggle as Paddy tried to heave himself up on the mattress. When he lost his footing, he fell back into the box with a little "oof" that sounded human.

Daniel groaned and flopped to his back. "You win, you swindler." He scooped the dog up and plopped him on the bed next to him.

Rose caressed his shoulder. "Thank you."

"I'll tell you this. He's staying on my side of the bed.

It'll be a cold day in hell when we sleep with a dog between us."

THANK THE GOOD LORD traffic wasn't as heavy on Saturday morning as on a weekday, Maureen thought as she gripped the wheel of the big Pontiac and inched toward Central Park West. And 'twas so nice of the motorcycle policemen to escort her over to Bridget's apartment house. She hoped she wouldn't sit in purgatory too long for the promise she made to the nice officers, that she'd park the Pontiac and not drive back to Brooklyn until early Sunday, when the traffic would be even lighter. Once she got rid of the police, she and Bridget would head upstate and make sure their children did the right thing.

The police had recognized Patrick's old car once she'd crossed into Manhattan. She hadn't noticed their flashing lights, but the sirens had finally gotten her attention. At first she thought it might have to do with the trash cans she'd mashed on her way out of the garage, but the officers hadn't mentioned those. They'd just offered to see her safely to Central Park. They'd even called in two more officers, so she had motorcycles to the front of her and motorcycles to the rear. Almost like a celebrity. She hoped Bridget was looking out the window. She'd be some impressed, she would.

ROSE AWOKE ONCE during the night and felt a cold nose against her cheek. It was not Daniel's. With a chuckle, she drifted back to sleep. The gruff, tough cop was a softie at heart, and she loved it.

The second time she awoke she smelled coffee—right under her nose. She opened her eyes and Daniel was passing a mug back and forth in front of her face, allowing the aroma to envelop her.

She smiled at him. "Good morning."

"Good morning, yourself." He set the mug on the bed-side table.

She eased up on one elbow. "Where's St. Paddy?"

"Eating breakfast. And he's been outside once already."

"Thank you, Daniel."

"You're welcome."

"You know, I probably dreamed this." She gave him a sly look. "But I could have sworn there was a furry body between us on the pillow last night."

"It was a dream. I have that puppy firmly under my control."

"Uh-huh." She took the mug from the table and sipped. "Mmm. Perfect. You're spoiling me, you know. I usually just throw a teaspoon of instant into a nuked mug of water."

"Not while I'm around, you won't. I've arrested people on less provocation than that."

She took another sip of the fragrant coffee and looked up at him from beneath her lashes. He was already dressed, but that could be remedied. "Did you bring your hand-cuffs, Officer?"

He folded his arms over his chest and gave her a stern look. "First you want a hickey and now you're talking handcuffs. Should I call in the vice squad, Rosie Kingsford?"

"Only if you can't handle the situation yourself."

He uncrossed his arms and approached the bed. "That sounded like a challenge."

"Are you up to it?"

He took the mug and set it on the bedside table before pulling back the comforter and tumbling her back onto the mattress. "I would say so. Consider yourself under house arrest." He pinned her beneath him.

"Is this how you subdue all your prisoners?"

"Only the sexy ones." He shifted his weight enough to slide his hand between her thighs.

Her breath caught as he began to explore and caress in a way that brought her to a fever pitch in no time. She pulled his head down. "Come here, you Irish stud." As she kissed him she fumbled with the fastening of his jeans. He caught her wrist and held it, keeping her from her task.

When she tried to twist out of his grip, he lifted his mouth from hers. "Don't seduce the cook."

"You're...cooking something?" she asked, breathing hard.

"Yeah. It's on low, but it'll be ruined if you get me involved in this little game. It's supposed to be your show this time."

"I don't care if the food's ruined."

His breathing had also grown ragged as he gazed into her eyes. "You know what, you sexy wench? Neither do I."

With a laugh of triumph she started to unfasten his jeans, but he moved her hand away.

"I can do it faster."

"Then do it, Daniel. Just do it."

And he did, marvelously. As he carried her to heights of passion she'd never known before, she barely noticed the smell of burned bacon drifting from the kitchen.

"YOU EMBARRASSED ME half to death, coming up to the apartment house with that entourage," Bridget said as Maureen drove along the shoulder of Highway 87 at forty miles an hour. "I thought the Pope himself had come to call."

"Oh, and I suppose you're used to the Pope driving up to your door for afternoon tea?"

"He might. It could happen."

Maureen gripped the wheel and concentrated on driving straight. "The day he wears underwear with shamrocks on it, I'd say."

"What are you thinking, talking about the Pope's underwear! That's plain sacrilegious."

"I never thought of it before, but do you suppose he wears briefs or boxers?"

Bridget groaned. "I don't want to consider the subject. Not for another instant."

"Boxers."

"I didn't hear that. And get off the shoulder and into the lane, for heaven's sake! You drive like an old lady."

"I do not! And you don't drive at all, now, do you? So you can stuff a sock in it, Bridget Hogan. I'm in charge of this vehicle."

Bridget held her head in her hands. "Jesus, Mary and Joseph. What have I gotten myself into?"

"If I remember right, your daughter is at the center of it, so don't be getting high and mighty with me. 'Tis your flesh and blood that's created the whole shebang."

"I put it all down to MTV. It's corrupted the morals of an entire generation. Maureen, you've simply got to drive faster. That man who just whizzed past made a very rude gesture at you."

"You mean he flipped me the Tweetie-bird, as Patrick used to say?"

"Maureen! I hope you don't use that kind of vulgar language on a regular basis."

"What's vulgar? Tweetie is just a cute little yellow canary. Even a person who lives on *Central Park West* should know that much."

Bridget stared at her. "When someone does that thing with their middle finger, it has nothing do with a little yellow canary. Trust me—Maureen! Not so close to the guardrail!" Bridget gasped and covered her eyes.

"You keep yelling and you'll make me nervous, you will."

"You *should* be nervous. I thought you said you could drive?"

"I'm driving!"

Bridget peered at her through her fingers. "Do you even have a license?"

"You didn't ask me that, now, did you?"

Bridget groaned again and crossed herself. "We're going to die. I'm going to be killed in a fiery crash, incinerated by the same woman who ruined my life. I guess that's fitting, after all. I should have known not to believe a woman who would soil a dear friend's reputation just because of a slight accident with a tanning lamp."

"Slight accident! I had second-degree burns, I did! Scabs on my nose!"

"You must have put the lotion on wrong."

"The lotion wasn't any good, and you well knew it."

"Did not."

"Did so."

"Did not."

"Liar, liar, pants on fire," Maureen said.

"I can't hear yo-o-ou," Bridget sang, covering her ears.

"I don't ca-are," Maureen sang back. She drove in silence for a couple of miles before realizing that Bridget was the one with the directions. "Are you going to tell me where to turn, then?"

No answer.

"You'd better tell me, or I'll just turn off any old place and park it."

"I—um—believe there was a grove of trees to the right of the highway when we turned. Yes, a grove of trees."

"But you don't really know, do you? Here we are on this wild-goose chase, and you haven't a blessed idea where the goose is!"

"I do so know! I'm just not...sure."

"I could wring your neck for you, Bridget Hogan. In fact, I think I will. I—"

"Don't take your hands off the wheel, for God's sake!"

"Ha!" Maureen replaced both hands on the wheel and increased her speed to forty-two miles an hour, just for the thrill of it. "Scared you, didn't I?"

"I saw my dear mother coming down from heaven to meet me. I saw the pearly gates and heard the voice of St. Peter. I—"

"Enough of that. Pick an exit. Any exit. I'm tired of this road and all these speeders rushing past me."

"I'll bet they're bloody tired of you, too," Bridget muttered. "There! I think that's the right one. And there's a grove of trees, too."

"There've been about ten groves of trees along this road, all as alike as peas in a pod. This one's no different."

"Turn off at this exit, Maureen."

"You'll probably have fetched us up in some cow pasture, but I'm turning." She swung the Pontiac in a wide arc and heard the screech of brakes behind her.

"You almost ran into somebody!" Bridget cried. "Don't turn so wide, Maureen!"

Maureen continued on. She was rattled, but she'd never let Bridget see it. "You know those signs on big trucks? The ones that say Wide Turns, Stay Back?"

"In case it escaped your notice, you're not driving a truck."

"I know, but next time, I'm getting one of those signs. Slap it right on the bumper, I will."

"There won't *be* a next time! You're a menace on the roadways."

"Am not."

"Are so!"

"Am not!" She turned her mouth up into a devilish smile. "Besides, I'm beginning to enjoy myself."

DANIEL HAD INSISTED on frying up a new batch of bacon to go with the eggs he scrambled with an expert hand.

Rose sat at the kitchen table watching him, her second mug of coffee in one hand and her other reaching down to scratch St. Paddy behind his floppy ears. "I don't remember when I've ever been so happy," she said.

Daniel flipped the bacon in the skillet and glanced over his shoulder. "That's how I like my food-poisoning victims. Happy and clueless."

"I'm beginning to suspect you're a pretty good cook."

"Self-defense. Most women I've met wouldn't be caught dead in a kitchen, and I like home cooking."

"And you thought I'd be different when I offered to make dinner on our second date. Sorry, Daniel. I hope that wasn't part of the appeal."

Dishing up a plate of bacon, eggs and buttered English muffins, he walked over and set it in front of her.

"Looks wonderful, Daniel."

He placed both hands on the table and brought his face close to hers. "For the record, your appeal had zero to do with your abilities in the kitchen."

"You just wanted to get me into bed."

He grinned at her. "Yep."

"A purely physical thing."

"Yep. And you were the same, Rosie. Admit it."

"I admit it." She cradled his face in both her hands and thought about her original intention to ask Daniel to father her child. Not *their* child, but *her* child. What a ridiculous idea. She considered confessing that stupid intention now, but she hesitated. He might laugh, but then again... The proposal sounded so crass in comparison to the wonder of what they'd found together, that she hated to risk injecting a sour note into the blissful harmony they'd created.

"And the physical part has been wonderful," she said. "But now..."

"It goes a little deeper than that," he murmured.

She gazed into his eyes. "Yes, it does."

He leaned closer to feather a kiss against her lips. "We should probably talk about that today." He pushed back from the table. "But let's eat this breakfast before it gets cold."

Yes, today, she thought. They'd plan their future and consider their options, meanwhile taking time out to make glorious love to each other. Smiling to herself, she unfolded her napkin and laid it in her lap. "I feel positively decadent, eating breakfast at nearly eleven in the morning."

"That's your fault." Daniel came over with his own plate of food and sat across from her at the small table. He took a forkful of eggs and paused with it in midair. "You weren't serious about the handcuff thing, were you?"

She laughed. "You really are worried that I'm the kinky type, aren't you?"

"No." He paused. "Well, maybe. When you get right down to it, there are lots of things we don't know about each other."

"It'll be fun finding out, then, won't it?"

"Yeah," he said warily, "as long as what we find out doesn't involve a cat-o'-nine-tails."

"Oh, Daniel," she said, still chuckling. "I think regular sex with you is going to be plenty exciting without getting into whips and chains."

He sighed with relief. "So you were kidding about the handcuffs."

"Yes." She chewed and swallowed a bite of food. "Sort of."

"Sort of?" He sounded nervous again.

"I've never known a man who owned handcuffs before." She winked. "We could, like, fool around with them."

He gazed at her, the light of arousal growing in his eyes. "I don't know how you do it."

"Do what?"

"You have that innocent look about you, but underneath, there's always a suggestion of..."

"Sin?"

"I suppose that's it. We have this perfectly good breakfast in front of us, and until two minutes ago I was starving. Now all I can think about is dragging you back into the bedroom."

"With handcuffs?"

"Yes, dammit! Probably with handcuffs, or a facsimile since I didn't bring any. You're turning me into an animal."

She smiled at him. "I have great material to work with."

He put down his fork and pushed back from the table. "I guess breakfast will be cold."

"I guess it will." She started to leave the table but paused in midmotion and cocked her head to listen. "That siren seems to be coming closer."

"I heard it, too. Probably old Tim running down another felon doing five miles over the limit. Right now I'm not much interested in old Tim's doings." He stood, his arousal evident from the bulge in his jeans. "Come with me, Rosie Kingsford."

She put her hand in his. "Daniel, that siren's really close."

"Must be on the road that goes past your lane. I—"

Frantic honking added itself to the increasingly loud whine of the siren. Both sounds filled the little kitchen.

Rose and Daniel stared at each other. Then, hand in hand, they walked into the living room and gazed out the window as a green Pontiac wheeled into the drive, followed by a squad car, lights flashing and siren wailing.

"Dear God," Daniel muttered.

"Do you know who it is?"

"I'm afraid so." He cringed as the Pontiac clipped his car's rear fender with a sickening thud before jerking to a stop in the mud next to the driveway. "It's my mother."

13

ROSE STARED at the Pontiac with growing horror as the passenger door opened. "And *my* mother," she said.

"Escorted to our doorstep by my old buddy Tim," Daniel added, heading toward the door. "My God. She could have killed herself, not to mention your mother and a cast of thousands."

Rose followed him. "I didn't know your mother could drive."

"She can't." He wrenched open the door. "If you noticed, she hit my car."

"I did notice." She followed him out the door.

Daniel started down the walkway. "She always did have a hard time figuring out which was the brake and which was the gas."

"This can't be real." Rose pinched her arm, hoping she'd wake up from this nightmare.

"Look on the bright side," Daniel said over his shoulder. "Tim will probably arrest them."

"Daniel!" She hurried after him. "We can't let Tim arrest our mothers."

"We might not have a choice. I hate to think of what your pretty little town looks like after my mother cut through it in that big Pontiac. I—" Daniel came to such an abrupt halt that Rose bumped into him. He spoke in a low, tense voice. "*Will you look at that?* He's putting his ticket book away. My mother talked him out of a ticket."

He started forward again. "I think I'll have a conversation with my bro Timmy."

Rose caught his arm. "You're going to ask him to give your mother a ticket?" she whispered.

"Hell, no. I'm going to protest mine!"

"Wait, Daniel." She kept her voice low. "We have bigger problems than your ticket. Let's act friendly, as if we're so glad to see our mothers, so glad to see Tim again."

"I'm supposed to be glad that my mother risked her life and Bridget's, smashed the fender of my car and corrupted a fine officer of the law?"

She decided not to point out that he'd tried to corrupt that same fine officer. "We won't get anywhere if we start yelling."

"I want to yell," he grumbled.

"Well, don't. Not until we find out what our mothers are up to."

"Just for you, Rosie."

"Thanks. Let me go first." Rose started down the driveway. "Mom! Mrs. O'Malley! How nice to see you." She wasn't encouraged by the frosty expressions that greeted her. "And good to see you again so soon, Tim."

"Just thought I'd escort these two ladies to their destination," Tim said.

Daniel stepped up beside Rose. "Sure gave them the royal treatment, using the lights and sirens and all. That's not what you usually see in your typical police escort, Tim."

Tim had the good grace to blush. "Well, actually, I did sort of want them to pull over, but I guess they weren't ready to do that."

Daniel's eyes widened as he turned to his mother. "You tried to outrun this patrol car?"

Maureen had a devilish gleam in her eye. "No trying about it. I did it. Patrick always did love that big V-8."

Daniel's expression darkened. "Mom, I ought to—"

Rose nudged him in the ribs.

"Don't worry about a thing, Daniel," Maureen said briskly. "I straightened it all out. You see, without your father, Officer Tim wouldn't even be here."

Bridget swatted her arm. "Don't say it like that, Maureen. It sounds like Patrick was fooling around with Officer Tim's mother."

"My Patrick? Never! What happened was Patrick took a bullet for Tim's father, before little Tim was even thought of. I just told Tim the whole story, so naturally he can't give a ticket to Patrick O'Malley's widow."

"What about Patrick O'Malley's son, Officer Tim?" Daniel asked, turning toward the patrolman. "You gave me a ticket, in case it's slipped your mind."

"I didn't know about the bullet thing then. I knew somebody had saved my dad's life a long time ago, but I didn't remember who it was." He brightened. "And now I do."

"And now that you do," Daniel said carefully, "what about my ticket?"

"Sorry, bro. I turned it in already. Now, if you want to come to traffic court, maybe we can work something out."

Daniel sighed. "Never mind. I guess the county can use the money."

"Which reminds me, old buddy. Your mom said you'd take care of the damage."

"You mean to my car?"

"No, it's the town welcome sign, with the population figure on it, and the founding date and all. I should say, it *was* the town welcome sign. Now it's pretty much firewood."

Daniel winced. "Anything else?"

"A couple of those whiskey-barrel planters that sit on the sidewalk along Main Street."

"They drove on the *sidewalk?*"

"Bridget distracted me. Yelling like a banshee, she was."

"Because you were headed straight for that bronze statue!"

"The damage shouldn't be much," Tim interjected quickly. "There weren't flowers planted in the barrels yet, and we were going to take that parking meter out anyway. And Mr. Webster may be old, but he hopped out of the way real fast. The sign's the main thing, but I'm sure you have insurance."

"Nope." Daniel leveled a scorching look at his mother. "Nobody expected that car to be on the road. Or the sidewalk."

Rose stepped forward. "I'll pay for a new sign."

"Oh, no, you won't." Daniel gave her a warning glance. "It's my mother."

"But, Daniel," Rose said, "that could be a very expensive item. I think you should—"

"I think you should just let it be," Daniel said quietly.

She heard the steel underlying his quiet statement and knew it was time to back off. This was one of their sore points, and now, of all times, they needed to stand together. "Okay."

"Get an estimate for a new sign," Daniel said to Tim. "I'll contact you soon."

"That's fine." Tim started backing toward his patrol car. "See you later, then." He seemed eager to leave.

Once the police car had pulled away, Daniel turned toward his mother. "What in hell were you thinking? You could have been killed!"

Rose knew his temper was past restraining and didn't attempt to stop the tirade that was sure to come.

"She almost killed us both!" Bridget said. "I was blessing myself so often I gave myself tendinitis!"

"I'm not surprised," Daniel said. "What do you have to say for yourself, Mom?"

Maureen's expression was unrepentant. "No grandchild of mine is going to be a bastard. Not while there's still breath in my body."

Rose's stomach felt as if she'd just jumped from a ten-story building. She gave her mother a panicked look and then she knew for sure. Bridget had sold her out.

Daniel stared at Maureen. "What in God's name are you talking about?"

"I wouldn't have believed you'd agree to doing such a sinful thing, Daniel Patrick O'Malley, but after I found out you lied about where you'd be this weekend, then I wasn't certain about anything anymore. This shameless woman just might have talked you into it."

Bridget grabbed Maureen's arm. "Don't you call my daughter shameless! You're the shameless one, running around looking for a wife for your rascal of a son."

"Hey!" Daniel said.

Maureen ignored him. "I thought she was a fine Irish girl!"

"She is!"

"She's little more than a—"

Whap. Bridget's roundhouse connected with Maureen's cheek and she stumbled backward.

"Mom!" Rose cried, starting toward her mother.

"'Tis another donnybrook you want, is it?" Arms flailing, Maureen headed back toward Bridget.

Daniel caught her before she made contact, and Rose grabbed Bridget.

Whatever hope Rose had that the whole incident could be smoothed over ended as Maureen turned to her son.

"So, have you agreed to give Rose the child she wants, without marrying her, then?"

Daniel's jaw clenched. "Look, that's enough. I have no idea what you're talking about, and you're doing nothing to help the—"

"Oh, so she didn't tell you her scheme, then? Never mind. Bridget was good enough to tell me. Rose doesn't want a husband, Daniel, but she does want a wee babe. You're chosen to be the father, whether she notified you of the fact or not."

"I don't believe you. Rose wouldn't want an arrangement like that."

Rose's heart broke.

"Ask her," Maureen prompted.

Daniel released his mother. Then he glanced at Rose, his expression confused. "She's got this all wrong, I know, but—"

"Not exactly all wrong," Rose said, her gaze pleading for understanding. "At one time I was looking for a man to father a child, although I didn't intend to marry him, or anyone, for that matter. I didn't want to go to a sperm bank and take my chances that the donor wouldn't be the sort I wanted, so I was looking for someone who would—" Her courage failed her.

His voice was strained. "Who would what?"

"Who would agree to give me a child without any strings attached."

"And you imagined I would?" The look in his eyes tore her to pieces.

"I...before I really knew you, I thought... But not after I found out what kind of man you are, Daniel. Being with you made me rethink everything! I would *never* consider such a thing now. Never.''

He grew very quiet. ''When did you change your mind about this? Be specific.''

''Sometime…sometime yesterday,'' she said.

''Before we gave St. Paddy a bath? Or after?''

She looked away. ''After.''

''How convenient. After you'd gotten what you wanted, you mean. No wonder you called me an Irish stud this morning. That's all I've been to you, isn't it?''

''No!'' Her face flamed. ''Daniel, not in front of our mothers, please!''

''A modern thinker like you shouldn't mind,'' he said, his tone icy.

Rose knew she was lost, totally lost.

''We're here to demand that you two marry and give our grandchild a proper home,'' Bridget said.

''In spite of the inconvenient matter of us two having to be related as a result,'' Maureen said with a shudder.

''Well, I hate to disappoint two such upstanding Catholic ladies, and I realize how much pleasure the union of our two families would give you, but I'm afraid it's out of the question,'' Daniel said. ''The prospective groom is too sick to his stomach to propose.''

''Daniel,'' Rose said. ''Please. Don't do this.''

''Oh, I think it's already done.'' He flicked her a glance. ''And you got exactly what you wanted. No strings attached. I won't even charge you a stud fee.''

FIFTEEN MINUTES LATER, Daniel left with his mother in the Pontiac. Rose agreed to drive her mother back in Daniel's car, then park it in his apartment garage and take a cab home. He didn't suggest she come up for a visit. He hadn't suggested that they ever see each other again, Rose noticed. Consequently, she had to postpone the drive back to the city until she could stop crying, which took a long time.

Eventually her mother started sniffling right along with her as they sat at the kitchen table. St. Paddy sat between them, his expression worried as his head swiveled from one tragic face to the other. Occasionally he'd whine and walk over to shove his muzzle against Rose's leg.

"I have to stop crying," Rose said, blowing her red nose. "I'm upsetting St. Paddy."

"St. Paddy? What about your poor mother? I'm a wreck!"

Rose glanced across the table at her mother's puffy eyes and red nose. "Yeah, you are."

"Thank you so much for agreeing with me on that. So you really love him, then?"

Rose nodded and choked back another sob.

"And if Maureen and I hadn't arrived and spilled the beans, you'd be setting the date?"

"I...I can't say that for sure. But we seemed to be...moving in that direction." Rose buried her face in her hands. "Oh, Mom. He's just what I want. I never thought I'd find a man who would make me change my mind about getting married, but Daniel did. And now..."

"It's all my fault." Her mother sounded completely miserable. "If I'd kept my nose out of it, everything would have been fine. Except, of course, for having to be related to that Maureen person."

"Don't blame yourself. I should have told Daniel the minute I gave up my original plan. He might have been upset then, too, but maybe I could have made him understand. Or maybe not. A man like Daniel would hate something like that. And that's exactly why I love him! It's so confusing."

Bridget reached over and placed her hand over Rose's. "The idea of being a single mother was never right for you, Rose. Motherhood is right for you, but so is having a husband. You only had to find the right man. Just because I didn't doesn't mean you can't. I was so young when I married your father. Too young to realize we had nothing in common but my good looks and his money."

Rose sighed. "Well, it looks like I've ruined my chances with this particular man, and I can't imagine there are many out there like Daniel O'Malley."

Bridget squeezed her hand. "Does he love you?"

"He was beginning to, I'm sure, but new love can be squashed so quickly. And I—well, I was having fun pretending to be a little wilder than I actually am. No telling how he's put all that together now, or what sort of picture he has of me."

"Rose, I have to ask you—" Bridget hesitated. "Considering what was said out in the front yard, could you be carrying Daniel's child?"

Rose's initial rush of joy at the thought was followed by great sadness. "I doubt it. I would love to be, but we—" She blushed furiously, but decided that if her mother had the courage to ask, she'd have the courage to tell. "We only had unprotected sex once. That would be quite a long shot."

"Ah, but he's an Irishman."

Rose laughed through her tears. "That's what *he* said."

"I think you should get in touch with him when we go back to the city. Convince him that you just weren't thinking straight about this other business."

Rose shook her head. "No. I did the pursuing in the beginning, and if I continue, he'll probably just think I'm after the same thing, because the first dose didn't take. I can't call him."

"That's your stubborn Irish pride talking."

Rose smiled at her. "I know I'm only half Irish, but it sure seems like the biggest half."

"Of course it is, lass."

Lass. She remembered Daniel calling her that, and how sweet the word had sounded coming from his lips. More such memories were undoubtedly on the way, and she was in for the kind of heartache she'd only imagined in the past. As they said in California, this was the big one. She blinked back fresh tears.

"I could call him," Bridget said.

Rose gasped. "No! Don't even think such a thing, Mom! You have to promise to stay out of this."

"But—"

"Promise me!"

"All right." Bridget slipped one hand into her lap. "I promise."

THE SILENCE in the Pontiac was oppressive, broken only when Daniel stopped for gas and asked his mother if she needed to go inside the station and freshen up. She declined. Daniel pumped the gas and swore softly to himself. On top of everything else, his mother had been driving on fumes. It was a wonder she'd made it to Rose's cottage without getting stranded.

They left the gas station and continued down the highway. Daniel flipped on the radio, but no matter how many times he switched channels he kept coming up with love songs. He didn't need love songs. What he needed, at least until the pain eased, was oblivion. But he had to take his mother home, and navigating a New York highway required his attention. Thinking of his mother driving this road froze the blood in his veins. She'd imagined she was doing it for him, so he'd decided not to say anything more about the stupidity of her actions. Next week, however, he was selling the car, fresh dents and all.

"You should be glad to know the truth, Daniel," Maureen said at last.

"Right."

"I couldn't let you go through with such a thing."

"I understand that."

"Daniel, what was it you meant when you said something about her getting what she wanted?"

Pain knifed through him. "Nothing."

"Could she be...carrying your child?"

Oh, God. If only— "Probably not."

"But there's a chance?"

"Not really."

"Don't be beating around the bush with me, Daniel. There's either a chance or there isn't. I keep up with these things. After all, products are sold out in the open now, you know, right next to my multivitamin tablets. You didn't use the sheepskin kind, did you? I read that those aren't as effective as latex."

Daniel blew out a breath. First he'd discovered that Rose was really after a sperm donor instead of a lover, and now his mother wanted to discuss his condom habits. He was so far past the end of his rope he couldn't even see it dangling there anymore.

"Well, Daniel?"

"You know what, Mom? We aren't going to have this conversation. Not now, and not in the future. Whatever did or didn't happen is between Rose and me. I once asked you to stay out of it."

"But when Bridget—"

"I can understand why you felt the need to warn me. Now I want the subject dropped. Permanently."

"Daniel, you're gripping that wheel as if you're likely

to bend it clean in half. Are you in love with that girl, then?''

"Drop it, Mom. Now.''

"All right. Mercy. I've never seen you like this. A body would think you'd tumbled head over heels.''

14

Inside the Statue of Liberty Museum, next to the big
foot. Noon, Tuesday. Be there.

                                                    B.H.K.

MAUREEN CHECKED the note again after boarding the ex-
cursion boat on Tuesday morning. She'd promised Daniel
to stay out of his business with Rose. But she hadn't promised not to visit the Statue of Liberty, had she, now? And
if she happened to run into Bridget there, and Bridget happened to mention the subject, was she supposed to clamp
her mouth shut and not answer at all? 'Twould be rude of
her.

She used to love this trip when Patrick was alive. There
was something wonderful about having a woman so huge
and magnificent at the entrance to one of the great harbors
of the world. Maureen had always thought the National
Organization for Women had missed a bet, not using that
statue as a symbol of female power.

And female power was just what was called for in this
mess surrounding Daniel and Rose. As the boat approached the giant copper figure, her torch raised to the
sky, Maureen moved to the front of the crowd and let the
wind blow against her face. Barbra Streisand had probably
felt like this in *Funny Girl* when she was singing "Nobody's Gonna Rain on My Parade," while riding that tug-

boat out into New York Harbor. Maureen's heart swelled with pride and purpose, and another emotion that surprised the devil out of her—sisterhood.

After the boat docked Maureen hurried to the museum. She knew the exact spot Bridget was talking about in her note. Inside the building was a huge left foot, reproduced the same size as the one on the actual statue, only 'twas polished copper instead of the weathered green of the statue outside. Maureen found Bridget standing by the big toe.

"So you came," Bridget said.

"Of course I came. Something must be done."

"Exactly. For our children and our grandchild-to-be."

Maureen laid a hand on her heart. "You really think Rose is in the family way, then?"

Bridget beckoned Maureen closer and leaned over to whisper in her ear. "They had sex once without a condom."

"Without a condom at all?" Maureen said in a normal voice.

Bridget clapped a hand over Maureen's mouth. "Jesus, Mary and Joseph. What am I to do with you, Maureen Fiona, shouting about condoms at the top of your blessed lungs?"

Maureen pulled Bridget's hand away from her mouth. "Did not."

"Did too."

"Did—" Belatedly Maureen heard the funny little tremble in Bridget's voice, and she looked her square in the face. 'Twas the moment she realized that Bridget was doing her best not to laugh, which set Maureen to giggling.

Once she started, Bridget joined in. Soon they were both gasping and holding their sides as tears streamed down their cheeks.

"No one could ever make me laugh like you, Maureen," Bridget said at last, wiping her eyes. "I don't think I've had a really good laugh since I left Ireland."

"We had some grand times, we did."

"I think...maybe we should forget about that Rose of Tralee business."

Maureen nodded. "I think that would be a grand idea."

"We have other fish to fry, like getting Rose and Daniel back together."

"'Tis not going to be easy. Daniel's a stubborn Irishman."

"And Rose is a stubborn Irishwoman, but I've figured out a plan. Rose will be riding in the back of a convertible during the St. Patrick's Day Parade. One of the beer companies hired her because she looks so Irish."

Maureen saw where the plan was headed. "Daniel will either be in it or patrolling a part of it, I'm not sure which."

"It would be best for my plan if he's patrolling a stretch of the route. If you'll tell me who his commanding officer is I'll have Cecil make a few calls and arrange it."

"Cecil? Your husband?"

"*Ex*-husband. But he knows a lot of people in high places here in the city. And even if he is a Brit, he wouldn't want his daughter to have a baby out of wedlock any more than I would. I'm sure I can convince him to help us set the trap for these two."

"You know, Rose and Daniel may well kill us for interfering again," Maureen said.

"I realize that. Are you ready to take that risk, Maureen?"

"I'm ready if you are."

"Then we must seal it with the secret handshake."

Maureen put her hand up, palm out, the memory as fresh

as if she'd done it yesterday, instead of thirty-seven years ago. Bridget placed her palm against Maureen's, and they laced their fingers together.

"All for one," Bridget said.

"And one for all," Maureen finished. Then she squeezed Bridget's hand tight. When she got an answering squeeze, she had the dumbest reaction. Tears filled her eyes.

ON ST. PATRICK'S DAY Rose wore a lined green suit with a white fake fur collar, which helped a little to keep her warm in the open convertible as it eased down the parade route. She rode on the boot covering the folded convertible top, which meant she was fully exposed to the chill wind that whipped down Fifth Avenue. There had been a long wait at the staging area, too. Although she'd thought the O'Hannigan's entry was near the middle of the parade, she'd discovered that morning that she'd been moved almost to the end. She'd been half-frozen before her part of the procession even got under way.

She'd tried to plan for the cold. Beneath her suit jacket she wore a thermal shirt, but there wasn't anything she could do about her legs. The suit skirt barely reached to mid-thigh, which had been exactly what the O'Hannigan's representative had wanted. He'd said something to the effect that a pantsuit would have defeated the purpose of hiring a woman with great legs. Rose had never liked being treated like a commodity, but after years of it she had become stoic about men like the O'Hannigan's rep. A set of earmuffs to cut the wind would also have been welcome this morning, instead of the perky green derby she wore securely pinned to her red curls, but O'Hannigan's Beer was paying a lot for her appearance in this parade, so she was expected to put up with a little discomfort in exchange.

Not long ago she would have been happy about the hefty fee offered by the brewery. She'd have rejoiced in her healthy financial situation, because it meant she'd be able to pursue her master plan more easily. Now her master plan was in tatters. She no longer cared about her little cottage, and drawing the comic strip was increasingly difficult these days.

Years of training were all that carried her through this morning as she smiled and waved at the crowd gathered along the parade route. She envied them their heavy coats and mufflers. March seventeenth had turned out to be a bitterly cold day in New York City this year. But as cold as it was outside, Rose was even colder inside. She'd hoped, prayed, even dreamed that Daniel would call. He hadn't.

Today, as if to mock her, she seemed to be surrounded by mounted patrollers. The contingent picked to lead the parade had been in the staging area, but Daniel hadn't been among them. More mounted officers were stationed along the route for crowd control. She'd studied each of them as the convertible inched down the street, but she hadn't seen Daniel. If she ever did spot him, she fully expected him to ignore her. How she'd keep smiling when that happened, she had no idea.

As the tail end of the parade approached St. Patrick's Cathedral, she glanced to her right and thought she recognized the man on the horse stationed in that block. Oh, God, it was him. She knew the set of those shoulders, the cant of those hips. Her heart began to pound.

Then, from her left, she heard a sickeningly familiar cry.

"I might have known you'd be here hogging the view, Maureen Fiona!"

She turned with a sense of inevitability to see her mother on the steps of St. Patrick's, trying to push Daniel's mother out of the way. Rose closed her eyes and prayed that the stress and the cold morning were causing her to hallucinate.

"Don't be shoving me, Bridget Hogan. 'Tis my corner you're standing on."

Laughter rippled through the crowd and Rose groaned. Maureen sounded like a streetwalker protecting her turf. Rose glanced toward Daniel to see how he was reacting. No help there. Daniel looked like a man chiseled in stone—his mirrored sunglasses concealing his eyes, a blue helmet over his dark hair, and his jaw set in uncompromising lines as he focused on the parade route and ignored the two women on the cathedral steps.

Rose leaned forward, as if that would make the motorcade move faster. But Murphy's Law was working overtime on this holiday, and the parade stopped altogether.

"Did you drive here, Maureen?" Bridget said, loud enough to carry a good half block. "I guess not, since I don't see your car parked on the cathedral steps."

"You know what I have to say to that? Take a look. The Tweety-bird is flying!"

"Oh, God," Rose muttered, her cheeks flaming as she imagined the private hell Daniel must be going through at the moment.

The driver of Rose's convertible chuckled. "Great show, huh? Nothing like a couple of Irish ladies going at it. Probably been drinking some of that green beer. If we're lucky, maybe they'll even throw a few punches."

Rose gasped at the prospect of the mothers becoming physical. Surely they wouldn't start a brawl on the steps of St. Patrick's Cathedral.

They would.

"I'll Tweety-bird you," Bridget said. "Take that, you sheep-faced old crone!"

"Missed me, you blind banshee!"

"I won't be missing you this time!"

As the blows started flying and the crowd made a circle around the screeching women, Rose clambered down from the back of the convertible, cursing her short skirt as she went. "Lean forward and let me out," she said to the driver. "I have to do something about this."

"Hey, it's not your business," the driver said, turning toward her. "Leave it to the police."

"I'm not going to debate this with you. Let me out or I'll climb over your lap."

Muttering something about the crazy Irish, the driver opened the door, got out and helped Rose down to the pavement.

"Thanks. I'll be right back." The crowd now blocked her view of the battling mothers, but all she had to do was follow the sounds of scuffling, shrill insults, and gleeful encouragement from the onlookers.

She shouldered her way through and made a grab for her mother. "Stop this right now!"

Bridget didn't even glance back at her. "Not yet, lass," she gasped. "Not until this is settled."

"Mom, stop!" Rose grabbed her mother around the waist, braced herself and pulled with all her might. It had no effect except that her skirt ripped up one side. O'Hannigan's would really get their money's worth now, she thought as she tugged harder. Then from the corner of her eye she saw the chest of a dark bay gelding part the crowd.

Daniel leaped from his horse and separated the two women with the same expertise he'd used in the apartment house lobby. For some unexplainable reason, the two women stayed separated this time. Daniel looked at his mother, opened his mouth to say something and closed it again, shaking his head.

Maureen's green derby was knocked askew, her coat was missing two buttons, and she was breathing hard. She was also smiling. "Don't stand there like a man with no tongue, Daniel," she said. "'Tis high time to speak to the woman you love."

With a startled cry, Rose stepped back and gazed at her mother, who was just as disheveled as Maureen and was also grinning like the Cheshire cat. "You two *staged* this?"

The crowd began to mutter and laugh among themselves at this new revelation.

"Had to do something," Bridget said. "Considering you were both too stubborn to contact each other."

Rose swung around to face Daniel at the same moment he turned to her. "I say we kill them," she said, her voice tight with fury. "No jury would ever convict us."

"Death is too easy for this pair," he muttered. "Let's torture them first."

"You've already been torturing us in grand style!" Maureen said. "Now stop your fussing and get married so you can give us both the grandbabe we're longing for."

"I couldn't have said it better, Maureen." Bridget walked over and put her arm around Maureen's waist. "I hope I didn't really hurt you. I was trying to be careful."

"Oh, *sure* you were," Maureen said with a chuckle.

Rose's knees felt suddenly weak. She glanced at Daniel. "This isn't real, right? Those are two aliens disguised as our mothers."

"Either that or they're both on drugs."

"Hey, buddy," called somebody from the crowd. "Looks like these two ladies went through a lot of trouble to bring you two together. You gonna propose to the young lady or not?''

Rose's heart began to hammer with a different rhythm. "Listen, Daniel, I—"

"Now don't you let him off the hook, Rose," Bridget said. "You told me yourself you love him, and Maureen's convinced he's in love with you. All you have to do is get him to tell you so."

"Tell her!" shouted an onlooker.

"Yeah, tell her!" called someone else.

The crowd turned it into a chant. *Tell her, tell her, tell her, tell her.*

In an agony of embarrassment, Rose covered her face.

The chant was ended with a blast from a police whistle.

Rose looked up as Daniel removed the whistle from his mouth. His expression was grim. He must be furious. This was really and truly the end of their relationship, thanks to one final stunt by her mother and Maureen.

Then a hint of a smile appeared on Daniel's face. "How do you expect a guy to propose with all that racket?" he called to the crowd.

Rose felt as if her heart had stopped.

A cheer went up from the crowd.

When it died down, Daniel turned to her and dropped to one knee. "Rose Erin Kingsford, will you marry me?"

"Oh, Maureen!" Bridget cried. "He's proposing on the steps of St. Patrick's Cathedral! It's perfect!"

There was a roaring in Rose's ears and she felt dizzy. She put out a hand to steady herself, and Daniel caught it firmly in his.

"I love you," he said in a low, urgent voice. "And I've been a proud, stubborn idiot. Marry me, Rosie."

She held onto his hand for dear life, afraid she'd tumble to the ground without his support. But she needed to see his eyes. "Take off those sunglasses," she murmured in a voice too low for the crowd to hear.

He pulled off the glasses. The depth of commitment in his eyes settled any doubts she might have had.

She spoke around the lump in her throat. "I would be honored to marry you, Daniel Patrick O'Malley."

"Oh, Bridget, I'm going to cry," Maureen muttered with a sniffle.

"Kiss her!" someone shouted.

"Great idea." Daniel got to his feet and pulled her into his arms.

"Daniel!" she protested, half laughing, half crying as she pushed at his chest. "Surely such goings-on aren't allowed when you're on duty."

The love in his gaze turned the chill day into a tropical paradise. "Ah, but 'tis St. Paddy's Day, and I'm Irish. Say you love me, Rosie."

"I love you, you crazy Irishman."

"That's all I need to know." As the crowd cheered again, he claimed the kiss she'd been yearning for all along.

Epilogue

MAUREEN HAD WON the coin toss to have the slide show of the trip to Ireland in her apartment, which meant she had to put up with Bridget's opinions on organizing her surroundings.

"I think you should hang the *Irish Rose* calendar on this wall next to your telephone," Bridget said. "That way you could see it whenever you made a call. And look at this! You still haven't framed your copy of the *New York Times* comic page. Anyone would think you didn't care that your daughter-in-law got her strip into such a prestigious paper."

Maureen checked on the lamb stew before turning to answer Bridget. "You well know why I haven't framed it. With the wedding, and our trip back to Ireland, and getting ready for the babe, I've been so busy I hardly have time to bless myself!"

"It's your lack of planning, Maureen. If you used your time better, you'd—oh, there's the buzzer. They're here!"

"Is the projector all set up?"

"Of course, although we have precious few slides to put in it."

"'Twas not me who dropped a roll of film into my Guinness."

"No, you were the one who started swaying while she sang 'My Wild Irish Rose' and bumped me."

"Did not."

"Did too."

"Did not!"

The buzzer sounded again.

Maureen placed her hands on her hips. "See how you do? You leave our poor children standing out in the elements while you fuss at me."

"It's your door! Go let them in, for heaven's sake."

Maureen lifted her nose in the air. "What a grand idea."

Shortly afterward Maureen was treated to the sight of her daughter-in-law, looking as if she'd swallowed a pumpkin, coming through the door with Daniel, who looked as if he'd swallowed a spotlight, he was glowing so much. While the stew finished cooking, Bridget showed the trip slides. Maureen never tired of looking at them, even if most of them were out of focus. She and Bridget had already made reservations to go back again next year.

Dinner was a success. Although Bridget complained as usual that Maureen's food was too fattening, she left a clean plate. Maureen was pleased to notice Bridget had gained a few pounds, too. She looked more content with life.

Over a dessert of Daniel's favorite chocolate cake, the talk turned, as it always did, to the eagerly awaited grandchild.

"Have you picked a name, then?" Maureen asked.

Rose glanced at Daniel.

"You might as well tell them," he said, scraping up the last of his cake with his dessert fork. "Get the haggling out of the way."

Bridget's spine stiffened. "Are you implying that we'll disagree with your choices?"

"The very idea," Maureen added. "'Tis your wee babe, and you can name it Elmer Fudd for all we care."

"But not Tweety-bird," Bridget said, and started to laugh.

"No, indeed." Maureen pressed a napkin against her mouth to stop her giggles.

"But I'm sure you've picked nice names," Bridget said. "What are they?"

Rose took a deep breath. "If it's a boy, we decided on Patrick Cecil."

"That's grand," Maureen said, dabbing at a sudden tear in her eye.

"I won't quarrel with your choice," Bridget said. "Cecil may be your father, but I agree he doesn't deserve top billing."

"And if it's a girl," Rose continued, "she'll be...Bridget Maureen."

"She's first?" Maureen cried before she could stop the words coming out of her mouth. "Did I lose the coin toss, then?"

Daniel cleared his throat. "We thought that was only fair, Mom. If the boy got Dad's name, then the girl should get Rose's mother's name."

"Well, I don't see the logic in it."

"Of course not," Bridget said. "But I think their reasoning is brilliant."

"We even tried to come up with a combination of your two names," Rose said.

"Yeah," Daniel added, "but Maurit and Bridgeen just didn't seem to cut it."

"I should say not," Bridget said. "They've done an outstanding job with the names, Maureen."

"That's easy for you to say. You're first in line. No, I think 'tis only fair to toss a coin. What do you say? Two out of three?"

"A coin toss to name a child?" Bridget said. "Next

you'll have us rolling dice to see which one gets to keep her the first time Daniel and Rose have an evening out.''

"'Tis no contest,'' Maureen said with a superior smile. "I already have a bassinet.''

"Well, *I* already have a stroller.''

"And I have a—''

"Oh, you know what?'' Daniel said. "We really have to go. Forgot to feed St. Paddy before we left.''

"Is that dog still sleeping in your bed with you?'' Bridget asked.

Rose looked sheepish. "We, ah, bought ourselves two new beds, one for the cottage and one for the apartment.''

"Oh, good,'' Bridget said. "And you're not allowing him in the new ones, are you?''

"Well, no. He sleeps in our old beds.''

Bridget rolled her eyes at Maureen. "Have you ever heard anything more strange than that? Giving up your bed to a dog?''

"Never,'' Maureen said. "I still can't believe they're keeping that dog in their apartment when they're in town. Frightens the neighbors out of their wits, he does. I—''

"And if we don't get back there soon,'' Rose said, "he just might eat one.''

Bridget gasped. "Would he do that?''

"You never know,'' Daniel said, and helped Rose on with her coat. After quick kisses all around, he escorted Rose out the door.

"I FEEL BAD maligning poor St. Paddy, who would never hurt a flea,'' Rose said as she and Daniel rode back to Manhattan in a cab.

"Me, too, but it makes them less likely to drop in on us, doesn't it?''

"Good point. You know, I think they took the name business rather well."

"If you mean no dishes were flying around, I guess you're right. Me, I'm hoping for a boy so we don't have to deal with it."

"Daniel, you know the ultrasound showed a girl."

"Maybe it missed something."

"I want a girl, anyway, and I want to name her after both our mothers. After all, this is all their fault."

Daniel caressed her round belly through the fabric of her maternity dress. "Not entirely. We had a little something to do with it."

Rose leaned closer to him so the cabdriver couldn't overhear. "And you really did know I was pregnant after that time in the bathtub, didn't you?"

"Not really. But I did know you were mine."

"You mean, like caveman stuff?"

"Exactly like caveman stuff. Staking my claim." He cupped her face in one hand. "And I feel like doing that some more...if you're sure the doctor said it's okay."

"It's okay. But, Daniel, your claim is well and securely staked."

"Maybe so," he murmured, leaning close for a kiss, "but I'll need a lifetime to be absolutely sure."

Harlequin Romance®

celebrates forty fabulous years!

Crack open the champagne and join us in celebrating Harlequin Romance's very special birthday.

Forty years of bringing you the best in romance fiction—and the best just keeps getting better!

Not only are we promising you three months of terrific books, authors and romance, but a chance to win a special hardbound 40th Anniversary collection featuring three of your favorite Harlequin Romance authors. And 150 lucky readers will receive an **autographed** collector's edition. Truly a one-of-a-kind keepsake.

Look in the back pages of any Harlequin Romance title, from April to June for more details.

Come join the party!

Look us up on-line at: http://www.romance.net

HR40THG2

MILLION DOLLAR SWEEPSTAKES
OFFICIAL RULES
NO PURCHASE NECESSARY TO ENTER

1. To enter, follow the directions published. Method of entry may vary. For eligibility, entries must be received no later than March 31, 1998. No liability is assumed for printing errors, lost, late, non-delivered or misdirected entries.

   To determine winners, the sweepstakes numbers assigned to submitted entries will be compared against a list of randomly, preselected prize winning numbers. In the event all prizes are not claimed via the return of prize winning numbers, random drawings will be held from among all other entries received to award unclaimed prizes.

2. Prize winners will be determined no later than June 30, 1998. Selection of winning numbers and random drawings are under the supervision of D. L. Blair, Inc., an independent judging organization whose decisions are final. Limit: one prize to a family or organization. No substitution will be made for any prize, except as offered. Taxes and duties on all prizes are the sole responsibility of winners. Winners will be notified by mail. Odds of winning are determined by the number of eligible entries distributed and received.

3. Sweepstakes open to residents of the U.S. (except Puerto Rico), Canada and Europe who are 18 years of age or older, except employees and immediate family members of Torstar Corp., D. L. Blair, Inc., their affiliates, subsidiaries, and all other agencies, entities, and persons connected with the use, marketing or conduct of this sweepstakes. All applicable laws and regulations apply. Sweepstakes offer void wherever prohibited by law. Any litigation within the province of Quebec respecting the conduct and awarding of a prize in this sweepstakes must be submitted to the Régie des alcools, des courses et des jeux. In order to win a prize, residents of Canada will be required to correctly answer a time-limited arithmetical skill-testing question to be administered by mail.

4. Winners of major prizes (Grand through Fourth) will be obligated to sign and return an Affidavit of Eligibility and Release of Liability within 30 days of notification. In the event of non-compliance within this time period or if a prize is returned as undeliverable, D. L. Blair, Inc. may at its sole discretion, award that prize to an alternate winner. By acceptance of their prize, winners consent to use of their names, photographs or other likeness for purposes of advertising, trade and promotion on behalf of Torstar Corp., its affiliates and subsidiaries, without further compensation unless prohibited by law. Torstar Corp. and D. L. Blair, Inc., their affiliates and subsidiaries are not responsible for errors in printing of sweepstakes and prize winning numbers. In the event a duplication of a prize winning number occurs, a random drawing will be held from among all entries received with that prize winning number to award that prize.

5. This sweepstakes is presented by Torstar Corp., its subsidiaries and affiliates in conjunction with book, merchandise and/or product offerings. The number of prizes to be awarded and their value are as follows: Grand Prize — $1,000,000 (payable at $33,333.33 a year for 30 years); First Prize — $50,000; Second Prize — $10,000; Third Prize — $5,000; 3 Fourth Prizes — $1,000 each; 10 Fifth Prizes — $250 each; 1,000 Sixth Prizes — $10 each. Values of all prizes are in U.S. currency. Prizes in each level will be presented in different creative executions, including various currencies, vehicles, merchandise and travel. Any presentation of a prize level in a currency other than U.S. currency represents an approximate equivalent to the U.S. currency prize for that level, at that time. Prize winners will have the opportunity of selecting any prize offered for that level; however, the actual non U.S. currency equivalent prize if offered and selected, shall be awarded at the exchange rate existing at 3:00 P.M. New York time on March 31, 1998. A travel prize option, if offered and selected by winner, must be completed within 12 months of selection and is subject to: traveling companion(s) completing and returning of a Release of Liability prior to travel; and hotel and flight accommodations availability. For a current list of all prize options offered within prize levels, send a self-addressed, stamped envelope (WA residents need not affix postage) to: MILLION DOLLAR SWEEPSTAKES Prize Options, P.O. Box 4456, Blair, NE 68009-4456, USA.

6. For a list of prize winners (available after July 31, 1998) send a separate, stamped, self-addressed envelope to: MILLION DOLLAR SWEEPSTAKES Winners, P.O. Box 4459, Blair, NE 68009-4459, USA.

You are cordially invited to a
HOMETOWN REUNION

September 1996—August 1997

Bad boys, cowboys, babies. Feuding families,
arson, mistaken identity, a mom on the run...
Where can you find romance and adventure?
Tyler, Wisconsin, that's where!

So join us in this not-so-sleepy little town and
experience the love, the laughter and the
tears of those who call it home.

WELCOME TO A
HOMETOWN REUNION

Daphne Sullivan and her little girl were hiding
from something or someone—that much was
becoming obvious to those who knew her. But
from whom? Was it the stranger with the dark
eyes who'd just come to town? Don't miss
Muriel Jensen's *Undercover Mom,* ninth in a
series you won't want to end....

Available in May 1997
at your favorite retail store.

 HARLEQUIN®

Look us up on-line at: http://www.romance.net

HTR9

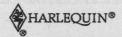

LOVE *or* MONEY?
Why not Love *and* Money!
After all, millionaires
need love, too!

How to Marry a MILLIONAIRE

Suzanne Forster,
Muriel Jensen
and
Judith Arnold

bring you three original stories
about finding that one-in-a million man!

Harlequin also brings you
a million-dollar sweepstakes—enter
for your chance to win a fortune!

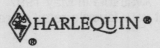

HARLEQUIN ®

MIRA Books is proud to present
the newest blockbuster from

DEBBIE MACOMBER

*"If I want to get married and have a family
(and I do!) it's time for a plan! Starting now."*
—Excerpt from Hallie McCarthy's diary

This Matter of Marriage

The Problem. Hallie's biological clock is ticking, she's
hitting the big three-0 and there's not one prospect for
marriage in sight.

Being an organized, goal-setting kind of person, however,
Hallie has...

The Solution. One full year to meet Mr. Right, her Knight in
Shining Armor.

But the dating game is always the same. One disaster after
another. Fortunately, Hallie can compare notes with her
neighbor, Steve Marris. He's divorced and in the same boat.
Hmm...too bad Hallie and Steve aren't interested in each other!

Available in April 1997 at your favorite retail outlet.

 MIRA The brightest star in women's fiction

Free Gift Offer

With a Free Gift proof-of-purchase
from any Harlequin® book, you can receive
a beautiful cubic zirconia pendant.

This stunning marquise-shaped stone is a genuine cubic
zirconia—accented by an 18" gold tone necklace.
(Approximate retail value $19.95)

Send for yours today...
compliments of ◈ HARLEQUIN®

To receive your free gift, a cubic zirconia pendant, send us one original proof-of-
purchase, photocopies not accepted, from the back of any Harlequin Romance®,
Harlequin Presents®, Harlequin Temptation®, Harlequin Superromance®, Harlequin
Intrigue®, Harlequin American Romance®, or Harlequin Historicals® title available in
February, March or April at your favorite retail outlet, together with the Free Gift
Certificate, plus a check or money order for $1.65 U.S./$2.15 CAN. (do not send cash) to
cover postage and handling, payable to Harlequin Free Gift Offer. We will send you the
specified gift. Allow 6 to 8 weeks for delivery. Offer good until April 30, 1997, or while
quantities last. Offer valid in the U.S. and Canada only.

Free Gift Certificate

Name: _____

Address: _____

City: _____ State/Province: _____ Zip/Postal Code: _____

Mail this certificate, one proof-of-purchase and a check or money order for postage
and handling to: HARLEQUIN FREE GIFT OFFER 1997. In the U.S.: 3010 Walden
Avenue, P.O. Box 9071, Buffalo NY 14269-9057. In Canada: P.O. Box 604, Fort Erie,
Ontario L2Z 5X3.

FREE GIFT OFFER   084-KEZ

ONE PROOF-OF-PURCHASE
To collect your fabulous FREE GIFT, a cubic zirconia pendant, you must include this
original proof-of-purchase for each gift with the properly completed Free Gift Certificate.

084-KEZ